"Shh... Tracy, tighter and ra... hair.

A tenderness he hadn't felt since ~~...~~ still alive kindled inside him. David wanted to release Tracy. He needed to release her, but *she* needed *him* right now.

She shook her head, her face still pressed into his shoulder. "No, it's not going to be okay."

David eased her from him and gripped her shoulders to look into her tear-reddened but still beautiful silver-blue eyes. "I'm so sorry about what you came across today, but Jay is going to be all right. And the police are searching for the guy who did this."

"You don't understand." Shaking her head, she moved away from him.

"Why don't you tell me, then? Is it the man who shoved Jay over today that has you upset and scared? Or is there something more?" The question sounded too personal, but he couldn't think of any other way to say it.

"Yes, there's more." Tracy stared into the fire.

"I'm listening. Tell me."

"I was the key witness in a murder trial. The killer on the mountain might be here for me."

Elizabeth Goddard is an award-winning author of over twenty novels, including the romantic mystery *The Camera Never Lies*—winner of a prestigious Carol Award in 2011. After acquiring her computer science degree, she worked at a software firm before eventually retiring to raise her four children and become a professional writer. In addition to writing, she homeschools her children and serves with her husband in ministry.

Books by Elizabeth Goddard

Love Inspired Suspense

Freezing Point
Treacherous Skies
Riptide
Wilderness Peril

Mountain Cove

Buried
Untraceable
Backfire

Visit the Author Profile page at Harlequin.com.

BACKFIRE

ELIZABETH GODDARD

HARLEQUIN LOVE INSPIRED® SUSPENSE

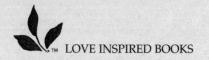 LOVE INSPIRED BOOKS

Recycling programs
for this product may
not exist in your area.

ISBN-13: 978-0-373-44674-2

Backfire

Copyright © 2015 by Elizabeth Goddard

www.Harlequin.com

Printed in U.S.A.

And we know that in all things
God works for the good of those who love Him,
who have been called according to His purpose.
—*Romans* 8:28

This story is dedicated to my Lord and Savior Jesus Christ—
who gave the ultimate sacrifice when He laid down
His life to save us. And to all the first responders, search
and rescue volunteers and firefighters, who give their time
and energy, face dangers of the worst kind, to help others.
I pray God's grace and many blessings for you.
Last, but never least, I dedicate all my stories
to my husband and children, who give me the time
and space I need to create stories, with a
special dedication to my daughter, Rachel, a real princess.

Acknowledgments

Many thanks to all my writing friends who have
encouraged me along the way, and a special thank-you to
Teresa Haugh for providing me with the important details
to keep this story true to the southeast Alaska setting. I
can't thank my agent, Steve Laube, enough for believing in
my work early on, and to my editor Elizabeth Mazer—
thank you for making each story the best it can be!

ONE

Mountain Cove, Alaska

Tracy Murray knew she had little time. A storm brewed in the distance.

But Solomon's urgent bark pulled her up the rising trail, indicating that there was someone in danger.

She sucked more air into her lungs that were already screaming from her workout.

Any other season on this trail—spring, winter, fall—she'd have to be concerned about the avalanche danger. But not during the summer, and because the season was so brief in Alaska, Tracy had every intention of enjoying the outdoors. Out for a run with her search-and-rescue golden retriever, summer abounded around her in the form of wildflowers and sundry small wildlife scurrying in and out of the flora.

Tracy had been heading for Keller Falls, four miles up the trail, until Solomon had taken off. She'd let him run free and hoped to practice a few commands. Up until a moment ago he'd run beside Tracy, surprisingly ignoring his natural instinct to chase forest animals, but then he'd taken off. With his continued excited and urgent barks, she knew that he had caught a human scent and was sending his vocal cue to alert Tracy that something was wrong.

Dread replaced the serenity she'd found on the trail.

Solomon was an air-scent search dog, wilderness search-and-rescue certified, and Tracy was still training him for both cadaver and avalanche certification. They'd already participated in several searches in the region as part of the North Face Mountain Rescue team. But Tracy hadn't taken her dog out looking for trouble today. No. She'd been looking for peace.

Instead her much-loved pet had likely found something. Or rather, someone.

Avoiding the steep and hazardous drop on the right side of the trail, Tracy kept running toward Solomon's sound-off. It surprised Tracy how far Solomon had gone on his own in the wilderness, but he'd obviously picked up a human scent that he intended to follow.

Though certified, Solomon was often eager to conduct a search even when he wasn't tasked with one, which frequently ended in false alarms—finding someone who wasn't lost. But if this was something more this time, at least she wasn't alone if she needed to call for help. She wasn't the only one who enjoyed an early morning run on this trail. Another runner had taken off on the trail ahead of her, and she'd run into David Warren heading the opposite direction on the trail, too.

He'd nodded and she'd nodded and they'd both given each other wide berth. Kind of funny now that she considered it. Living in Mountain Cove for two years, Tracy had worked with the firefighter on several search-and-rescue missions, but he seemed aloof. A few years older than Tracy in his late thirties, the man still attracted plenty of female attention with his rugged appearance and strong, lean body. His smile was the kind that turned heads and could make a woman weak in the knees.

Despite all that, he wasn't married, didn't have a girl-friend, and Tracy knew why—he was too cold on the inside. Even if he wasn't, she'd have kept her distance because of his profession. Tracy wanted to avoid any reminders of the night that had changed her life forever. Any reminders of what had sent her into hiding.

Make that who.

And that was one reason she'd chosen to live in Mountain Cove. Surrounded by temperate rain forest in Southeast Alaska, the chances of seeing a wildfire were next to zero.

She shook off the unwelcome thoughts and focused in on Solomon's alerts. His barks came from the area to her right, which was nothing but a steep ridge. Her heart sank. She'd purposefully avoided that ledge. How had Solomon found his way down? Or had he fallen?

God, please, no.

"Solomon!" Tracy crept to the edge and peered out over the rocky, jagged escarpment, part of the gorge that originated at Keller Falls. Where was he?

The drop was steep, terraced with granite or bedrock in places, and it was on one of those natural terraces that Solomon stood barking. Fear gripped Tracy. How could she bring Solomon back up?

"Solomon! Come," she called.

The position of his ears and tail signaled that he'd found someone who was injured or scared. Solomon peered up, his brown eyes somber, and when he saw her, he lay on the small space—a signal to mark the spot. But where was the injured person?

Then, just beyond a bush growing from the ridge, she spotted a body. Tracy's pulse thundered in her ears. The

breath rushed from her—it was the man who'd run ahead
of her. But Solomon hadn't signaled that he was dead.

And then the man lifted a hand and called out to her.
He wasn't dead after all, but he'd taken a fall. How had
he survived?

Tracy could barely hear his cry for help.

"I'm calling for assistance," she yelled down to him.
"Just hang in there!"

A chill slid down her spine. The sense that someone
watched crawled over her. Phone in hand, she called for
help for the fallen jogger while she scanned the woods
behind and around her.

A man stepped out of nowhere and Tracy gasped—
then let out a sigh of relief when she saw it was David.

But the sense of unease didn't disappear.

And she still had a feeling she was being watched.

Breathing hard, David bent over his thighs before gasping out, "I heard the dog, wanted to see if there was a
problem." David wiped the sweat from his eyes, sucked
in a few breaths to slow his breathing after he'd sprinted
up the trail then cut through the woods.

Phone to her ear, Tracy stared at him with those big
silvery-blue eyes of hers, the terror slowly fading away
to shock and concern. What was going on?

Scrunching her freckled nose, she glared at her phone.
"Lost the signal. Oh, I don't have time for this."

"What's wrong?"

A deep frown crossed her features as she shoved the
thick red hair from her face. "I'm so glad you're here.
A runner fell. He's down there." Urgency in her voice,
Tracy paced as she pointed to the steep, rocky drop. "He
needs our help."

David peered over the edge and spotted Solomon—

how had the dog made it down there?—and just beyond he saw the hiker. The man was still alive? Apprehension lodged in David's gut. How long had he been there?

Pulling his own phone out, he looked for the bars. "Got 'em. Use my phone to call for help. I'll climb down to him." David was assistant chief of the Mountain Cove Fire Department and a paramedic. He spent most of his time as a firefighter answering EMS calls rather than fires, and he had too many SAR certifications to count. He was well qualified—he just wished he was better inventoried. Out on his morning run, he had no medical equipment or emergency supplies. All he could do was assess the man's injuries and reassure him while they waited for help to arrive.

Reaching over, Tracy pressed her hand against his arm, uncertainty in her eyes. "Be careful. You don't even have your climbing gear."

He'd gone on enough free-soloing climbs—free climbing with no ropes—to know this ridge wouldn't be a problem for him. "Don't worry. When you reach someone, tell them we'll need a helicopter to hoist this man out. That fall had to have severely banged him up." If he wasn't mortally wounded.

David suspected the latter but wouldn't voice his concerns because Tracy was already on edge. She'd seemed unusually distressed. In their previous interactions, the experienced search-and-rescue volunteer was always in control of her emotions. Was there more to this than she'd admitted?

Before he climbed down to the injured jogger, he needed to know. "Did you see what happened?"

She shook her head. "Like you, I followed Solomon's bark. He took off ahead of me."

David eyed the dangerous ledge, deciding on the safest and quickest path to the man. He started down, with one last glance up to Tracy, and noticed her looking behind her as though she expected someone to jump out of the woods.

Gripping the rocks, he paused and called up. "Tracy."

His short, snappy tone got her attention.

She peered down at him. "What?"

"Did you reach anyone?"

"I'm on hold."

"Figures. Are you going to be okay?" He should be more concerned about the fallen runner, but he couldn't shake the sense that something had scared Tracy. Or was he just being an idiot?

"Of course. Why wouldn't I be?"

He shrugged and continued down.

Tracy had caught his attention the first time he'd met her a couple of years ago. She'd just moved to Mountain Cove, she'd explained after he'd run into her coming out of his brother Adam's bicycle shop. Collided, more like, and he'd had to assist her off the ground—her and the new bike she'd purchased. He should have offered to buy her coffee or something. Any normal red-blooded male would have. With her thick, red mane and deep, striking eyes, he hadn't stopped thinking about her for weeks after running into her.

Maybe he was just lonely. Starved for female companionship. But he didn't think that was it. There was just something about Tracy. But getting involved wasn't for him anymore. Yeah, he saw how happy two of his siblings—Heidi and Cade—were now that they had each finally gotten married. Cade and his wife, Leah, had had their first child two months ago, naming him after their late father, Scott Daniel Warren. And Heidi had married Isaiah, a family friend, SAR volunteer and a coworker at the avalanche center that their father had founded. David's siblings had done well for themselves.

He'd known that kind of happiness once. But he'd lost it; let it slip through his fingers. He didn't deserve it again. His wife had died in a fire when he, a decorated firefighting hero, had failed to save her. How could he have let that happen?

He didn't deserve happiness. Not after that. And after Tracy had snagged his thoughts with one run-in, he knew to keep his distance from her on their search-and-rescue missions and training events. And even when he saw her in town.

He reached Solomon and petted the dog, giving him plenty of reassuring verbal rewards.

"I'm on my way down," he called to the injured man. "Hold on."

The trim man looked to be about average height, healthy except for the way he lay twisted at an angle a few feet below the narrow ledge where David and Solomon now stood. He likely had a few if not many broken bones and possibly had internal injuries, as well. David was astounded he had survived, and if the rescue helicopter didn't arrive soon, he might not make it.

Carefully gripping the rocks, David inched his way down.

Finally he reached the narrow terrace and looked down into dark gray eyes filled with pain and fear. "My name's David. I'm a firefighter and paramedic. Lie perfectly still. Help is on the way."

Kneeling beside him, David assessed the fallen man's wounds the best he could, but with a possible spinal injury, David avoided moving any part of his body. Blood oozed from a gash in the man's head, coagulating in his light brown hair. David removed his own jacket and then his T-shirt, using it to apply pressure to stanch the flow. He could do at least that much. He cringed to think of what was going on inside the injured man's body.

"It's pretty bad, isn't it?"

"You're going to make it."

God, let my words be true. Save this man, help him.

The man closed his eyes.

"What's your name?" David had to keep him awake, keep him talking, if he could.

"Jay Woodall."

Maybe David couldn't offer much physical assistance, but emotional and mental encouragement was just as important.

Clouds brewed in the distance, forecasted to bring a torrent, and David could already smell the rain. Lightning flashed and thunder rolled, warning of the storm's imminent approach and leaving David unsettled. They didn't usually get thunderstorms. He sure hoped that helicopter got here soon. He didn't want to see Jay suffer any more by getting soaked and chilled on top of his injuries.

"Why?" Jay's croak resounded with the shock of his trauma.

Recognizing the man's emotional distress over his predicament, David frowned. Was he asking why God would allow him to fall? David had enough of those questions himself. Questions he'd never resolved since he'd lost Natalie. He feared it might take a lifetime to find the answers, or worse, that he never would. He fought to keep from railing at God on some days. But he shoved his inner turmoil aside to focus on the here and now and the man who needed his help.

David might not be able to answer those kinds of questions, but maybe he could help in other ways if he knew more. "Can you tell me what happened?"

"Someone…pushed me over. Tried to kill me."

The news stunned David. Did Jay know the person who'd done this?

David glanced up the rock-faced cliff and spotted Solomon watching. From here, David couldn't see Tracy. He wished Solomon would find his way back up to her.

Was Jay's attacker still up there? If so, Tracy was up there alone with a dangerous man—a man who'd attempted murder.

TWO

Tracy ended the call.

Help was on the way, but would it get here before the storm? Wind whipped around her and the trees swayed. A sound caught her attention from the thick woods behind her. Woods she'd enjoyed only moments before. But now the dense tangle of trees had turned dark and sinister, as though hiding a secret.

Or a killer.

She rubbed her arms to chase away the chill that crawled over her. She was being ridiculous. If only David hadn't sprung from the woods like that and startled her. Her heart still pounded from the scare he'd given her. That was all this was about. There wasn't a bogeyman standing in the shadows. She didn't have to be afraid anymore. The only people who had any reason to want to harm her were thousands of miles away and had no idea where to find her.

She peered down the ledge. David was with the injured man, holding his hand and offering gentle reassurances. She couldn't hear what they said from there, but could tell the man, broken as he was, had relaxed somewhat.

Maybe David wasn't as cold as she'd thought. From here, she could barely make out his chuckle. Probably telling the man a funny story or joke to get his mind off his injuries. Glancing up at the sky, she tried to gauge whether help would arrive before the storm. She knew how difficult it could be to execute rescues in stormy conditions, but this man would die without immediate help. As the sky grew darker, so did the woods.

Again that sense that someone was watching slinked over her and kept her on edge. Tracy hated her paranoia, but she had good reason.

Tracy looked behind her again, watching her surroundings to reassure herself no one was there. Normally she had the comfort of knowing that Solomon could protect her if there was anything to worry about. But how to get the dog back from where he'd traveled down the ledge? She called him, using the command he should quickly respond to, but he wouldn't move from his perch. She had no idea if he simply wasn't able to make the climb—though she hadn't seen him try—or if he was committed to the fall victim.

There was nothing for it. Tracy would have to climb down to him. She was an experienced climber herself and had paid attention to David's path down, but she couldn't see herself going all the way to the fallen jogger without climbing gear. Again she searched for the path Solomon had taken, but saw nothing, at least from this angle.

She eased herself down and, her feet and hands gripping the rock face, pressed herself into the granite, taking in quick breaths. She hadn't ever done this solo—without the ropes in case she fell. But it wasn't that difficult. Solomon had picked his way down without climbing somehow, so she knew she could, too.

She sent up a quick prayer and continued to make her way until Solomon was only a few yards below her. When fear crept in, she imagined she had the necessary ropes and gear to keep from falling and continued on.

The next thing she knew, hands gripped her waist.

"You're almost there," David said. Relief flooded her as David assisted her the rest of the way. She could have done it without him, but it was a comfort to know he was—literally—watching her back. But why had he felt it necessary to leave the fallen runner?

When she turned her back to the rock face she'd just scaled, David stood mere inches from her.

Much too close.

"What…what are you doing? Why did you leave him down there alone?"

"I needed to check on you, too."

"I'm a big girl. I know how to take care of myself." His nearness and concern confused her. Putting space between them, Tracy knelt next to Solomon and hugged him to her. "Good boy."

"The man's name is Jay Woodall, by the way."

David studied the ledge above as if looking for that same bogeyman she had feared moments before. Or maybe more help.

"Oh, now I can see how Solomon found his way, David." Tracy pointed to a place a few yards to the right that connected with the trail farther down. There were enough rocks and outcroppings for the dog to stair-step his way. "Solomon and I could go back up and wait for the SAR team coming on foot. We can show them the easier way down, while you wait with Jay for the helicopter."

"No. You and Solomon should stay here, where I can see you."

"David." Tracy stood as he turned to face her. "What's going on?"

"Somebody pushed Jay over."

The news punched her gut. Tracy gasped and cupped her mouth, stepping back.

"Watch it." David caught her and pulled her away from

the ledge. He gripped her arms. "I don't know why some-one would do that, but we can't know if they're still lurking in the woods somewhere and waiting for their chance to finish the job."

"You have a gun, right?" Tracy expected he carried some form of protection with him when in the woods in Alaska, as did most people. Bears were the main threat. Tracy had her bear spray, but somehow it didn't make her feel secure if she had to face off with a killer of the human variety.

His features twisted into a half frown, half smile. "Yeah, even when I'm jogging. But don't worry. I can't believe anyone would do something like this and hang around for long. We'd see him for sure."

Tracy nodded. Solomon could warn them, as well. Jay was fortunate that she and Solomon had been on the trail when they were. People often told her Solomon's breed didn't make for a good guard dog, but he'd saved her life once. She'd trust him again.

"I want you to go down and wait with Jay," David said a moment later. "I'm going to check the trail and make sure it's safe for the incoming SAR team."

"I'm not as good a climber as you. I don't think I could make that."

"It's not that far. I'll go down first and if you can ease down a few inches I can almost reach you."

When David moved to scale the cliff the rest of the way to Jay, Tracy grabbed his arm. "David."

"Yeah?"

"Thanks for coming back to check on me."

"Of course."

His gaze lingered on hers longer than necessary. She wasn't sure why, but unfortunately, she liked it. What was it about him?

Then he turned his attention to the climb down. She couldn't have known when she woke up this morning that the day would end with her taking refuge on a small terrace in a cliff face with Solomon, a fallen jogger and David Warren, hiding from a would-be killer.

Tracy waited with Jay while David climbed up to make sure it was safe by the trail for the incoming SAR team. The guy had courage and was all about protecting others.

He leaned over the ledge and looked down at her now to let her know he had finally returned. The clouds chose to release their burden at that moment, lashing them with a relentless fury and forcing her to drag her eyes away from the ledge.

At least the rain woud keep her from looking up every other minute, terrified that the next person she saw would be the man who'd shoved Jay over the ledge.

How was it that she had to face off with a killer twice in her life? She wanted to question God about the insanity in this world. Wanted to condemn David for leaving her. Solomon, too.

As it was, she feared Jay was quickly losing his battle with death. But she was thankful David had returned. She never thought she'd ever be so glad to see him—a man she'd avoided.

She looked up again and saw David. His gaze held hers as the rain pounded all of them and he shouted, "I'm coming down."

"What about the rocks? Won't it be too slippery? Maybe you should wait," she called up.

"I have gear this time. SAR is here." He shot her a smile and gestured with the climbing ropes before he started setting an anchor. But then he frowned. Called down to her. "How's Jay?"

Tracy's heart lurched. "Not doing very well, I'm afraid."

He made it about halfway then called down to her again. "You pray, Tracy?"

She'd prefer he paid more attention to rappelling in the rain than trying to reassure her.

She wished she had a hood. Something. Rain splattered her face when she called up. "Yes, of course."

"Well, good, then. Because we have that, if we have nothing else. And it's what truly matters."

Tracy had seen the Warren family in church; heard they were heroes and Christians. But she hadn't known the depth of that conviction until now, when David gave her a glimpse of the man he really was on the inside.

And then he was right next to her, holding her steady in the pouring rain.

He pulled the pack from his back and took out a big sheet of plastic. "Here, take this for a minute. I'm going to hold this over you and Jay to cover you."

He also tugged out a thermal blanket. "Now, cover Jay. At least we can keep him from getting any wetter. Keep him warm."

Tracy nodded and did as David asked.

Jay's eyes blinked open. "Why did this happen?"

"I'm sorry... I don't know. But there is a helicopter coming. It'll be here soon, Jay. You're going to be just fine." She didn't want to ask if he was in pain because she knew he was. "As soon as the helicopter gets here, the SAR team will position you in the rescue basket and the medics will take care of you."

God, please let the rain stop, just long enough for us to get Jay to safety. Airlifting someone injured could be treacherous on a good day, much less in a rare thunderstorm.

Why had this kind of weather unleashed now, with Jay straddling this world and the next?

"What happened, Jay? Why'd someone push you off a cliff?" Tracy cringed. Should she really be asking him? It wasn't her business. Those questions were for the authorities.

Still, it creeped her out to think that Jay's would-be killer had been lurking in the woods. Maybe if she understood what had happened, she wouldn't be so scared.

"Saw him on the trail. Stopped to catch my breath. Just making conversation. Then he tried to kill me." Jay coughed. "Probably thought he succeeded. That's what I get for being too friendly."

Tracy had nothing else to say but that she was sorry, and she didn't want to say that repeatedly. Nor did she like the sound of his cough. Maybe he shouldn't even be talking. She opened her mouth to tell him that he should rest now when he spoke again.

"He had an interesting tattoo. I've been thinking about getting one…and I asked him about it. Maybe that's what sent him into a fit. How crazy is that?" He squeezed her hand.

But it was as if he squeezed her heart. Tracy couldn't breathe. Images of the worst night of her life filled with flames and smoke and death accosted her. Somewhere outside her memories, David asked if she was okay, but she couldn't escape the images.

"Tattoo?" she finally managed to ask. "What…kind of tattoo?"

Jay closed his eyes. Was he unconscious again?

"Jay, please, I need to know. It could help us identify the man who did this."

She held her breath, afraid she would never get the answer. Fearing what the answer might be all the same.

The pounding rain slowed to a trickle, giving them a reprieve. In the distance she heard the whir of the rescue helicopter.

The plastic David held shifted. "Tracy," he said. "I need you to climb back up to give us room to get Jay on the rescue basket and into the helicopter."

Still reeling over what Jay had said, she couldn't respond.

"It's safe, Tracy. Others are up there. The Mountain Cove PD is on the way, too."

He lowered the plastic. "Tracy? Are you okay?"

"Sure. Give me a sec." She squeezed Jay's hand, trying one last time. "What kind of tattoo, Jay? Please, it's important."

He looked at her then, the pain in his face almost intolerable. "Numbers and a scorpion with flames on the wrist. I should have known better, but I thought it was cool. Asked what the numbers—"

Tracy didn't hear more, having already gone into a shock of her own.

No, it couldn't be…

How had he found her?

THREE

The helicopter hovered above them.

David stood underneath the rescue basket that was used like a medical stretcher, watching as Jay was hoisted up and into the chopper. The rain was beginning to lash them again. Carefully securing Jay in the basket without complicating his injuries had been a difficult task and had required the SAR team and the expertise of the flight paramedics working together. David was also a paramedic, but he was tired and drained and had stepped back to let the fresh crew on duty do their jobs. However, Jay had wanted him there, holding his hand, making it a tight fit on the rocky terraced outcropping.

David said a silent prayer that Jay would fully recover. All things were possible with God. Like Jay being found to begin with. The helicopter swayed unsteadily in the wind, and lightning flashed. This was one of the most hazardous rescues he'd participated in.

And he hadn't even been on call. He'd just happened upon the situation, or rather, Tracy had happened upon it. Her search-and-rescue dog had been the one to alert her, and David had heard the dog's bark in the distance. He hadn't even thought twice before he'd turned around and run back up the trail to find Tracy and Solomon.

Despite his severe and potentially lethal injuries, Jay would live—that much David believed to his core. The guy was a survivor and had a strong will to live. Once he had been lifted and secured, the helicopter carried him away on the flight of his life.

The adrenaline rush that had kept David going bled out of him, and he realized he was chilled to the bone in his rain-soaked running clothes, minus his T-shirt, of course. But there was one more mission David needed to complete. One more person he needed to see to. Tracy had never left his thoughts.

The SAR members that had helped with the extraction—David's brothers, Cade and Adam, and their brother-in-law, Isaiah—had already climbed back to the trail. David followed them up, making his way slowly and meticulously in the rain, bringing the climbing ropes with him. When he'd come here for a quick run before the storm he could never have imagined this day would turn out this way.

When he finally reached the trail, David discovered Tracy had already gone. But what had he expected? For her to wait in the rain for him? Not to mention there was a would-be killer out there. Unless the police had caught the guy, no one was safe on the trail. Besides, why would she wait for David? It wasn't as if they had ever been anything beyond acquaintances until today. And even now, David wasn't sure they'd inched any closer to an actual friendship. That was why his disappointment surprised him. But on the other hand, he was glad she had gone.

The torrent had begun again. David didn't bother to make conversation with Isaiah, Cade and his younger brother Adam. Instead they trudged their way toward the trailhead.

David tried to process everything they'd just been through, including Tracy's reactions, which unsettled him in some way he couldn't quite define. They just didn't make sense. It was normal that she'd been shaken by the idea of an attempted murder, but there was more to it than that. David hadn't been able to hear her conversation with Jay over the noise of the rain beating down on the tarp he'd held, but he was sure that whatever it was Jay had said had shaken Tracy. But what could it have been? David shrugged the question off. He wouldn't be getting any answers to it out here.

Finally the rain let up again. David hoped it would stay that way until he was inside his truck with the heat on.

Isaiah stepped up next to him. "The police showed up and escorted Tracy and Heidi back. They were going to take Tracy's statement about the fallen jogger and what she'd seen."

"Are you saying they didn't search the woods?" David asked. "Just took a statement?"

"I'll talk to Terry and see what I find out," Cade said.

Terry served on the Mountain Cove PD. He and Cade had been close since grade school, though Terry was a friend to all the Warren siblings. David would ask Tracy what she'd told the police, as well.

They made the trailhead where their vehicles were parked. Isaiah and Cade scrambled into Cade's truck, Adam into his own vehicle, and David climbed into his shiny, brand-new, blue Ford Super Duty F-250 FX4 4x4. He loved his truck and was glad he'd special-ordered it, though that had required a wait. But if he'd been trying to fill the empty space inside with material goods, he knew he'd failed. For whatever reason, the incident this morning seemed to drive home his loneliness.

He waved at his brothers then turned on the ignition and the heat. Dripping wet, he shivered and stared out the window, recalling what had happened.

The fear he remembered from Tracy's expression told him that something was terribly wrong.

Considering the way their brief encounter had affected him the first time he'd met her, David had made it his policy to steer clear, never involve himself with her. He shouldn't get involved now, but he couldn't stop thinking about her reaction. Couldn't stop thinking about her. He wanted her to be safe, but he knew it went much deeper than that.

He was more confused than ever.

Finally at home, Tracy gave Solomon a much-needed bath and fed him. Then she took a hot shower to wash away the events of the day as well as the chill from her body, then put on a pot of coffee to brew. She needed to stop her shivering limbs. But as she slipped into her comfortable, warm sweats, she was still shaking. The real source of her trembling had nothing at all to do with getting chilled on the mountain.

No. Her trembling had everything to do with the strong possibility that Carlos Santino had somehow found her.

The tattoo that Jay had described was the tattoo worn by Santino and his gang members.

Fear crept over her again as she recalled Jay's words.

"Numbers and a scorpion with flames on the wrist… I thought it was cool. Asked what the numbers—" Tracy knew what those numbers meant. She knew more about that particular tattoo than she'd ever wanted to. Every kind of gang—ethnic or otherwise, street gangs or prison gangs—had their coded tattoo system and tattoos symbolizing membership.

The scorpion and flames identified Santino's gang, and the numbers identified how many kills. As that number grew, other tattoos would tell the story elsewhere on the body.

But Santino was supposed to be in a prison in California—over a thousand miles away. As far as she knew, no one in this region of Alaska had even heard of Carlos Santino or his gang…except for her.

How could that be a coincidence, especially when you threw in Jay's attempted murder? Had he finally found her so he could pay her back for her testimony against him? He'd threatened her, warning that he would find her and kill her with his own hands. And that had sent her running.

Hiding.

There was only one thing to do next. Find out if Santino had escaped. Tracy dug through the drawers in the old rolltop desk that came with the cottage, her nervous fingers creating a mess of the contents and making it more difficult to find the card she needed. She should have memorized the number. But she'd wanted to put that part of her life as far behind her as possible. Find some normalcy.

Lord, why did this happen?

She huffed a laugh. She was asking Jay's question now. She hoped they would both get answers.

There. She gripped the corner of the card at the very back of the drawer. Of course. Tracy slid it to the front and lifted it from the drawer. The insignia at the corner was a marshal's badge similar to those worn in the Old West movies, only this one had an eagle embossed over the top of the badge. It read "US Department of Justice, United States Marshals Service." Then "Jennifer Hanes, Deputy US Marshal" was printed beneath those words.

Jennifer would have handled Tracy's transfer into the

WITSEC program if Tracy had chosen to go that way. She had told Tracy to call her if she ever needed her.

Tracy's hand shook so much, she couldn't read the number. She placed the card on the desk. Though she dreaded the call she had to make, Jennifer would be able to give her answers. The problem was Tracy wasn't sure she wanted to hear what the woman had to say. Still, she needed to know if Santino was still in prison or if he had escaped.

She moved around the cottage until she found a good signal and made the call. It went to voice mail and Tracy left a quick message. She didn't detail what had happened; only asked if Santino was still in prison.

"Please call me back," she said. "Something's…happened."

Tracy ended the call. She had thought she'd never talk to Jennifer again. She hadn't imagined she would ever have to. Setting the phone on the desk, she admitted that she'd really just hoped and prayed she would never have to contact Jennifer again.

The call made, there wasn't anything more Tracy could do until she heard back. She'd told the Mountain Cove police everything that had happened today. Everything except about her past and why she'd come to Mountain Cove. Telling them a killer could have followed her here when she was still considered relatively new to the community might make her look like a troublemaker. She'd been afraid to take that risk.

Though she'd lived here only a couple of years, Tracy loved Mountain Cove, and up until today, she had thought she'd found a place she could finally call home. She could never go back to live in Missouri, where her family lived, or Sacramento, where she'd worked as a newspaper editor and where she'd met Derrick. Where all her troubles had begun.

Of course, if Santino had actually come after her here, then she needed to tell the police everything so they would understand what they were up against. She wondered if other law-enforcement entities would get involved, too, swarming down on Mountain Cove. Then the community would wish they had never seen Tracy Murray.

At the moment all she needed was time to think things through. Then if she confirmed it really was Santino she would proceed according to plan, whatever that was. Unfortunately, she didn't know where else she could go.

How could anyone have found her here?

In the old comfy chair by the fireplace, Tracy tugged her knees up to her chin and watched the flames. Even though it was summer, the evenings were cold enough in Mountain Cove, Alaska, to justify lighting the fire. Soaking in the warmth, she tried to calm her nerves. Until she received a return call from Jennifer she would be on edge, trying to figure out what to do next.

She lived rent-free with Solomon in a small cabin as part of her pay for working at Jewel of the Mountain Bed and Breakfast. The job and her living situation had fallen into place so easily after her arrival and had made her feel as though she was exactly where she was supposed to be. Finding Mountain Cove in the first place had been providential. It was the perfect place where she could hide as well as train Solomon for search and rescue. And it was so far off the beaten path, so distant from the world she'd known before, that she'd felt completely hidden and totally secure. But after the events of today, it didn't appear to be far enough away to keep her safe. There was still a chance that her testimony, given years before, would get her killed.

She hadn't been the only witness to Santino's crimes, but the other guy had taken the get-a-new-life card and run with it straight into witness protection. He'd left everything behind to escape having to live his life in fear that Santino would come for him one day.

A knot grew in Tracy's throat and lodged there. Had she made a mistake by choosing to stay out of the program, trying to keep from losing everyone else she loved? Hadn't losing Derrick been enough? Had her decision backfired on her?

Though Tracy had feared for her life during Santino's trial, and the potential retaliation should he be convicted, her biggest fear had been losing her family. Her father had refused to change his name and move the family to start a new life with her. He'd refused to be forced away from the life he loved, surrounded by lifelong friends and extended family. He'd refused to leave behind the oil business he'd built. That wasn't something he could easily build up again elsewhere.

And Tracy had refused to leave her family behind— never seeing them again. Never making contact. That kind of price was too high for the added security of witness protection. It was as though she was the one being punished for doing the right thing.

Instead, Tracy had moved to Alaska, to a place that couldn't even be approached by car. A person could reach Mountain Cove—in the Inside Passage of Southeast Alaska—only via floatplane or boat. Hiking in was out of the question.

And this way, she could still go see her family anytime she wanted, while protecting herself by being almost completely isolated from the rest of the world. Yes, in a way she had in fact run from her life and was in hiding after a fashion, but it wasn't quite as severe as the other choice.

And it wasn't quite as secure, either. As today had proved, there was still the chance that she could be found and her life could be put in danger again.

Tracy paced the room, rubbing her arms, forcing down the bile rising in her throat.

When would Jennifer call back? Tracy wanted to know Santino's status. If she had internet she could search the news feeds and find out. Maybe. But she didn't. Part of the allure of the Jewel of the Mountain Bed and Breakfast was that people were forced to enjoy nature—there wasn't anything else to do, and that, according to Jewel Caraway, the owner and Tracy's boss, made the place the perfect getaway.

Solomon rested by the fire, and Tracy crouched next to him, ran her fingers through his thick, golden fur. "You did well today."

She leaned closer to him. He wasn't a trained attack or guard dog, but she knew that Solomon would protect her better than just about anything else. Or anyone. He'd already proved that once, the night that Santino had burned down her house. The same night he'd burned Derrick's house to silence him forever. Solomon had been able to save Tracy.

A growl erupted from Solomon and his ears perked up. In that moment he wasn't the typical overfriendly golden retriever. No. Solomon was protective of Tracy and he sensed a possible threat. Tracy stood, her gaze flickering to the windows and the door. Fear corded around her throat.

But when she heard the telltale sound of someone approaching the front door, she ran her hand down Solomon's back to reassure him. "Bad guys don't knock."

No. Bad guys push people off ledges. Burn down their homes while they're sleeping. Find good people where they hide in order to kill them.

FOUR

David stood at the cottage door, his knuckles ready to knock. He took in a breath. What was he doing here? Tracy probably wouldn't appreciate the intrusion. And David was conflicted about whether he wanted to be here, too. He'd set his boundaries and now he was taking a step outside that imaginary line.

But Tracy's welfare was much more important than David's need to protect his heart. That was it, then. He wouldn't stand on the sidelines and do nothing. If there was a way he could help he would.

He knocked on the door.

Behind it, he heard Solomon's bark. He couldn't tell if it was a friendly bark or not.

Better identify himself. With a potential killer on the loose out there, he might have startled Tracy. But she wouldn't expect Jay's attacker to knock.

"Tracy, it's David Warren."

He heard the lock disengage and then the door opened. Tracy stood on the other side and eyed him, a tenuous smile on her lips. He could see the questions in her eyes. And along with the questions, that same fear in her gaze that he'd seen on the mountain today.

"Hello, David. What are you doing here?" She held on to the doorknob.

A short laugh escaped him when he realized he didn't really have an answer for her. He'd thought this through so well. *Way to go, David.* "Checking on you."

Solomon pushed through from behind her and came up to sniff David. He leaned to run his fingers through the dog's fur, rub him down. "Hey, boy," he said softly.

With everything that had happened today, he wondered if anyone had told Jay about the dog finding him. Or if Jay had been coherent enough to hear the dog's barks and know how he'd been discovered.

"Why do you think you need to check on me?" Her free hand trembled.

Why indeed? He pulled away from the dog and stood tall, scraping his hand around the back of his neck. He turned to the side and peered through the trees toward the house at the front of the property, noticing the lights were on at the main building of the bed-and-breakfast. He turned his gaze back to Tracy. Might as well be transparent.

"I can see something's wrong, that's why." With each second, he felt more like an idiot. Of course there was something wrong. They'd helped a man today who had nearly been murdered. David should just turn and go. She didn't want him here. Even though he could easily see something was wrong—she was scared to death—he wasn't the one to help.

Just as David opened his mouth to apologize for disturbing her evening, Tracy opened the door wider. "Please come in. I have coffee brewing, if you'd like a cup."

"Thanks, I'd like that." He stepped inside the warm and comfy cottage.

Her simple invitation and the offer of coffee made

him happier than it should. He wasn't here to explore a relationship with Tracy. In fact, he wanted to avoid one at nearly all costs. But Tracy's safety was not one of the costs he was willing to pay.

She moved to the small kitchen area against the wall and grabbed two cups. David stood in the middle of the cozy main room and took it all in. She'd made the cabin her own, with quilts hanging on the walls. On the rocking chair hung a partially completed rainbow afghan. A fire glowed in the fireplace, chasing away the chill brought on by this afternoon's storm and the approaching evening. But as comfortable as the room was, David felt awkward and wasn't sure how to proceed.

Tracy moved to the kitchen table that sat only two and set the cups there. She poured coffee into both. "Cream or sugar?"

"Black is fine, thanks."

She appeared to feel as awkward as David. What was it between the two of them? He didn't have this much trouble feeling comfortable with any other person in town.

"Sit down. Make yourself comfortable."

He did as she asked while she went back to the fridge for half-and-half. She poured it from a glass container and again he noticed how shaky she seemed. Then she dropped the glass.

It shattered on the floor, the crashing sound slicing through the awkward silence.

Tracy just stood there and stared, her whole body shaking.

David was up and next to her in a second. "Don't worry about this. I'll clean it up."

His gaze shot around the room, searching for where she might keep her broom and cleaning supplies. What he really wanted to do was just take her in his arms. He'd do that for anyone else who was as obviously upset as she was. Why couldn't he do that for Tracy? What was the matter with him?

Then she covered her face and her shoulders shook.

Oh, boy.

David pulled her away from the glass on the floor and into his arms. Of course, he knew this breakdown had nothing at all to do with the fact she'd dropped the cream container. That event was simply the catalyst to shred her poised veneer, which David knew had been shaken already.

She sobbed into his shoulder, igniting all those protective instincts inside his heart for her. Having her in his arms this way, her tears accosted the wall around his heart. If he wanted to protect himself, he'd leave before her vulnerability had the chance to obliterate his defenses altogether. But what could David do? He was here now. He had to see this through.

"Shh… Tracy, it's okay." He hugged her tighter and ran his hand down her red hair against her back, trying to stay focused on just reassuring her and nothing more.

But a tenderness he hadn't felt since his wife was still alive kindled inside him. David wanted to release Tracy. He needed to release her, but *she* needed *him* right now.

Her sobbing finally spent, she shook her head, her face still pressed into his shoulder. "No, it's not going to be okay."

A shudder ran over her. What in the world?

David eased her from him and gripped her shoulders to look into her tear-reddened but still beautiful silver-blue eyes. "I'm so sorry about what you came across today, but Jay is going to be all right. And the police are searching for the guy who did this."

She sniffled and pulled away from him to grab a tissue from the counter. He knew he should be glad to have some distance between them again. It was crazy that he wanted her back in his arms. They burned, his chest burned now, where she'd been pressed against him. The girl was more caustic to protecting his emotions than he realized.

"You don't understand." Shaking her head, she moved farther away from him and grabbed a broom and dustpan from a small closet.

David went ahead and picked up the bigger pieces, careful he didn't cut himself handling the glass.

"Why don't you tell me, then?"

Tracy swept the glass into the dustpan and disposed of it. Then she pushed her hair away from her face and behind her ears and turned her big eyes on him. "All right. I'll tell you."

He didn't know why, but her willingness to talk startled him. The fact she trusted him with whatever it was made him happy, though it shouldn't.

"I was surprised to see you at the door, honestly." She grabbed her cup of coffee and instead of sitting at the table moved to the small sofa, curling her legs under her.

He was surprised he'd come himself, but he wouldn't tell her about his inner struggles.

Not wanting to sit too close to her, David took the kitty-corner chair. He also took a sip of the black coffee, still trying to regain his composure. She'd been upset and she'd transferred all that to him, it seemed.

"Is it the man who shoved Jay over today that has you upset and scared? Or is there something more?" The question sounded too personal, but he couldn't think of any other way to say it.

"Yes, there's more." Tracy stared into the fire.

David had suspected there could be more going on

from the beginning, but hearing her say the words unsettled him.

"I'm listening."

She dragged her eyes from the fire and studied him. "And that's why I'm going to tell you. I never thought I'd be talking to you like this. Or telling David Warren, of all people, my troubles."

What was that supposed to mean? But he swallowed his pride and kept quiet.

"But you showed up at my door, and there is no one else for me to talk to. I'm waiting for a phone call from the only other person I can talk to about this, and she hasn't come through yet. My family... I can't tell them what happened today. I don't want to scare them, worry them."

"Tell me."

"I was the key witness in a murder trial."

David set his cup down on the side table. "You have my attention."

"Jay's attacker might be here for me. He might have come to Mountain Cove to kill me."

Tracy couldn't stand to see the stricken look on David's face. He shoved himself up from the chair and paced the homemade rug in front of the hearth. His sturdy form seemed to further diminish the size of her small cottage.

She rubbed her eyes, hating that she'd lost it with him. For all practical purposes, he might as well have been a stranger. But, no, that wasn't right, either. She'd known him, just from a distance. And that had all changed today. Why of all people had David Warren come into her life here and now? During this crisis?

"I can't believe this." His voice was gruff. "How do you know? How can you be sure? If that's true, why did he shove Jay and not wait for you to come up the trail? Or why didn't he shove you when you found Jay?"

David stopped pacing and stared at Tracy. She had a question, too. Why did David care so much? The urgency in his tone made it sound as if he cared like someone deeply connected to Tracy. A father. A brother… A husband. She shook off the thoughts. This was crazy. She needed an ally, but at the same time, David was risking his life by getting involved with her. Maybe she should just refuse his help, his friendship.

Tracy frowned. "I don't know if I should answer any of your questions. In fact, I don't think it's a good idea that you're here. Being with me only makes you a target. I need to be alone." If only she wasn't so desperate. If only she didn't need someone.

Tracy had moved here to be more isolated, and she'd been wary of making friends until enough time had passed. She had only started growing closer to Jewel, her boss. That had been a mistake. David being here was a mistake, too.

He stalked over and sat next to her on the sofa, too close for comfort. "You're kidding, right? If there really is a killer after you, you can't go through this alone. I assume you told the police what you told me?"

She shook her head. "Not…yet."

He stiffened. "We need to call them."

"I've put a call in to my contact at the US Marshals office. She'll know if Carlos Santino has escaped prison. That will tell me what I need to know—that he's out and after me."

Oh, no. Tracy grabbed her head, fisted her hair. She'd been so focused on Santino's threat—that he would kill her with his own hands—she hadn't realized what should have been obvious. Santino's long arms could reach her from prison via the gang network.

Santino didn't have to be out of prison to be after her. Still, she had to know if Jennifer knew if something was going on; had to know if Santino had escaped.

"Tell me what Jay said to you that made you think his attacker is after you."

David's nearness, the protectiveness pouring off him, was difficult to resist. More than anything, Tracy wanted to feel his arms around her again. She would never forget that moment, but the problem was, she couldn't afford to dwell on that. To wish for something more with him.

"Carlos Santino is the head of a far-reaching gang and Jay told me the guy who pushed him over had a specific tattoo—it is the tattoo worn by those gang members."

There. She'd told him everything. Almost. Tracy stood to put space between them and went to the fireplace.

Behind her, she heard nothing at all from David. Maybe he was absorbing it all, which she understood. That could take some time. Or maybe he was contemplating the quickest escape from her and her problems. She wouldn't blame him for that. She wouldn't blame him if she heard the door shutting behind her, but she realized that probably wouldn't happen. If she knew anything about David, it was that he was a solid, trustworthy sort of guy.

Tracy turned to face him then. He was right behind her and she hadn't realized he'd moved from the sofa.

"Listen," she said, "I didn't mean to drag you into this. I won't hold it against you if you bail."

"Are you in the witness protection program, Tracy? Is that even your real name?"

A sardonic laugh escaped. "No, I'm not. And, yes, Tracy Murray is my real name. What does it matter? Did you hear anything I just said?"

"Why aren't you in WITSEC?"

"I chose not to run and hide—well, other than to Alaska."

"If this guy is so dangerous I think you need to get help and disappear. Let the Marshals office assist you with that."

Seeing the concern in his eyes, Tracy couldn't help but smile. "You know, we're only just getting to know each other and you're already trying to get rid of me."

Oh, please, she did not just say that.

He cracked a smile, though only half his face responded.

She liked that look on him.

"I'll be up-front with you," he said. "I'd like to get to know you better, but not at the risk of your life. I'm sorry it took me this long to say more than two words to you, but that doesn't matter anymore. You need to disappear. Where's the number? I'll call them and tell them what happened and how important it is to keep you safe."

David was definitely a take-charge kind of guy, thinking his words would move Jennifer to take action. And his words confirmed to her why she loved Mountain Cove so much. The sense of community here. People cared. She couldn't afford for them to care for her, but still, she didn't want to leave. Didn't want to run again.

"I've called my contact. Left a message. Until she calls me back there's nothing more that I can do." There was nothing he could do, either.

"Sure there is. You can get out of here."

"And go where?" She almost yelled the question at him. She moved away from him, which was increasingly difficult to do in this cottage that seemed to grow smaller by the minute.

At the kitchen sink, Tracy washed out the cups and

the coffeepot. She doubted either of them would drink the rest.

"Anywhere would be safer than staying here."

"I'm in the middle of nowhere, practically, David. People can't even drive here. You know that. If someone can find me here, they can find me anywhere. So…no." Well, that was it, then. She had made up her mind, thanks to David. "I'm not leaving. I refuse to have someone else control my life anymore. I won't be forced out of a life I love, a town I love. I'm just like my father after all."

David took the cup from her and placed it in the cabinet. "Your father?"

"Yeah, when I first agreed to testify, I told my family that we could all go into WITSEC. He refused to go into the program with me. He has a successful business he doesn't want to leave behind. He can't start his life over. I couldn't leave my family behind like that, never to see them again. I'd already lost so much." Lost someone she loved. "So instead of entering the program, I dropped off the map on my own. And I love my home now. I'm staying here."

"Okay, then, it sounds like you've made up your mind and I can't convince you otherwise." Something in David's tone pulled her attention from washing out the sink and up to his earthy green eyes. "And believe me when I say that I don't want you to leave."

Tracy wanted to go into his arms. The oddest of things—she'd spent half a day with the man and here she was, wanting to feel his arms around her. She shook off the foolishness his proximity brought on and took a step back.

"I'm not really sure what to say to that."

He laughed. "At least sleep in the house with Jewel and her guests until they catch this guy, okay? And if you don't already have a weapon, then get one."

Stay in the main house and put Jewel and the others at risk? No, she couldn't. "I have Solomon to protect me, to warn me. He saved me before, so I trust him to do that again." And she had the big can of bear spray and the smaller pepper spray she carried in her purse. But her excuses sounded weak, even to her own ears.

David didn't appear convinced, but it wasn't his decision. And yet Tracy cared about his opinion and she wished that she didn't.

"You really think Solomon can protect you from a killer? Maybe he saved you before—I don't know the circumstances. And maybe he can warn you, but, Tracy, even if Solomon was a real guard dog, he couldn't protect you from this guy. And what about the danger to *Solomon*? What if the man has a gun next time? Solomon doesn't wear armor. What if he gets hurt trying to protect you?"

Tracy hadn't thought of it that way, and the accusation in David's tone choked her. But she didn't get a chance to respond. Her cell phone chirped. Tracy rushed to the end of the counter and stared at the caller ID. The number on the screen belonged to Marshal Jennifer Hanes.

FIVE

The next day Tracy was still thinking about her phone conversation with Jennifer as she bought a few groceries and necessary items. She couldn't stay holed up in her cabin, turning it into a self-made prison because of what had happened. After her shift at Jewel's this evening, she'd needed fresh air. Besides, she would soon run out of the basics, such as shampoo, toothpaste and soap—not to mention food. She could eat up at Jewel's but she didn't like to overstep.

And now it was nearing ten o'clock at night and the sun had set about half an hour ago. She had another half hour of twilight or so, at least, but the sour expression on the store clerk's face made it clear that she wanted Tracy to leave so she could close out her register and lock up the store.

She reached for the half-and-half to replace what she'd dropped last night right in front of David. That had been the catalyst that had sent her into his arms. Wonderful, strong arms. And from there she'd ended up telling him nearly everything.

Her hands weren't shaking now, but the danger was still there. She could feel it closing in on her, despite what Jennifer had told her.

The woman's words drifted back to her now.

"Santino is still incarcerated, Tracy. I haven't heard any chatter on my end to lead me to believe members of his gang have any intention of looking for you to exact revenge. They're busy focusing on running guns and drugs and fighting the law down here in the Lower 48. Honestly, there isn't enough information to go on from what you've told me. Other than WITSEC, there aren't many options for you, if you're concerned about your safety. But I'll tell you what I will do. I'll contact the local police chief in Mountain Cove to bring him up to speed with your particular situation. But let's not escalate things unless it's warranted. You could still be safe there. Please call me if you need me. And, Tracy, remember, per our agreement, the door is still open for you to enter WITSEC."

Though relieved that Santino was still in prison, and the fact that Jennifer sounded unconvinced his gang had come for Tracy, she felt a little let down by the conversation. She wasn't sure what she'd expected Jennifer to say or to do. But if Jennifer believed Tracy was in danger, at the very least Jennifer should try again to convince Tracy to let the Marshals office assist her into a new life. Maybe this time Tracy would listen. She'd mostly wanted Jennifer's reassurance and she'd gotten that, but for some reason it didn't make her feel any better.

Admittedly, Tracy's story didn't sound all that credible, even to her own ears. But she couldn't shake the feeling that Jay's attacker—whoever he was—had come to Mountain Cove for her.

She'd give Jennifer enough time to speak to Mountain Cove's police chief before she went in to talk to him, too. That way, they'd take her seriously.

She finished paying for her few groceries and toiletries and gave Veronica, the store clerk, a big smile, hoping to defuse any hard feelings because she'd shopped beyond the ten o'clock closing time. She hated shopping so late and then having to drive back out to the B and B, but Jewel had kept her late tonight.

Tracy hadn't found a way to tell Jewel her story yet. She wasn't sure how she would react to the news, and Tracy needed more time to figure things out. What if Jewel fired her, fearing Tracy had brought danger to her door? Then she really would have no options. And yet it wasn't fair to keep her boss and friend in the dark, either.

God, what do I do?

Her thoughts went immediately to David and his concern for her. She had a feeling that he would throw a fit if he knew she was here alone at the grocery store at this hour, though it wasn't his business. He knew everything now—well, almost everything—and the previous day, he'd acted as if he might stand guard over her cottage until the end of time if she hadn't run him off. He'd been so concerned about her, and she'd wanted to shake what that did to her insides.

She was still much too raw to put herself in that kind of heart-risking, vulnerable position again. Now that she knew him a little better, there was no doubt that she could fall for a guy like him hard, but caring about him would put him in danger. Caring about him would also be a liability to her heart.

She couldn't afford to get involved with him. Still, she admitted that, deep inside, David Warren gave her just another reason to want to stay in Mountain Cove.

A noise like cans being knocked over sounded at the back of the store. The clerk looked up from assisting Tracy with her groceries.

"What in the world?" Veronica said. She shook her head. "And I wanted to get out of here early. I have to work tomorrow, too."

"I'll help you stack whatever it is back up. After all, it's my fault you're here so late." Tracy smiled.

"You'd do that?" Veronica eyed her.

"Sure. Why not?" Tracy waited for Veronica to lock the front door. Then, leaving her groceries at the counter, she followed the clerk to the back.

Cans of green beans that had been on the endcap for a promotional sale were scattered everywhere. Veronica blew out a breath. "Can't imagine how this happened."

The look she gave Tracy was a little accusing. "Don't look at me. I didn't buy any green beans. Didn't even touch them."

Another sound—garbage cans tumbling—resounded from outside the back exit. Tracy stiffened. She headed to the back of the store and immediately felt a rush of cold air. The back door wasn't closed completely. She and Veronica had been alone in the store. But it looked as though someone had entered through the back, accidentally knocked the cans over and then sneaked back out. Or maybe Tracy's imagination was getting the best of her. Still, she didn't want to risk it. "Veronica, you should call the police."

Veronica stooped over to grab a few cans and stack them. "Look, that would mean I'd get out of here after midnight and I sort of had plans. It's nothing. A cat or something. The wind. Could even be a bear messing with the garbage."

"What about the cans?"

"Someone didn't stack them right to begin with."

"Are you sure?"

"I'm positive. Wouldn't be the first time. I appreciate your help with the cans."

Tracy went to the back door to secure it. Hands against the panic bar, she considered opening the door to look outside into the alley. But that could be inviting trouble if there had been a bear messing with the garbage or if a creature of the two-legged variety was out there.

No. Tracy wouldn't open the door. She tugged it closed completely, which should automatically lock this kind of door. Then she helped Veronica with the cans. When they'd finished, Tracy grabbed her two bags of groceries and Veronica let her out the front door so she could close out her register. Tracy didn't like the situation at all, but maybe she was being paranoid. Veronica hadn't thought anything of the cans or the noise.

But Veronica didn't know what Tracy knew.

Outside a lone fluorescent light in the parking lot flickered on and off as darkness tried to settle on the short Alaska night. Her old junker Corolla was parked at the far corner. It had been the only spot left in the small parking lot when she'd first arrived. The place had been full of people making that last run for a quart of milk before it was too late. And Tracy had hung around too long, too lost in thought to concentrate on her shopping. But she hadn't thought this part through.

She didn't relish walking the parking lot alone even if it hadn't grown completely dark yet. She wished Solomon had come with her, but folks didn't usually like to see a dog in the grocery store unless it was a service animal. Tracy needed assistance of another kind.

There was nothing for it—she had to get to her car. She couldn't stand here all night. She started off across the parking lot, but that sense that someone watched her crawled over her. Just like on the mountain. If someone had come here to kill her, why didn't they just get it over with? Why toy with her or play games?

Juggling her groceries, Tracy pulled out the small can of pepper spray she kept in her purse, just to be safe and prepared.

And after tonight, she'd take David's advice and get a weapon. Learn to use it to protect herself. He was right. Solomon couldn't fight off all threats, especially if he wasn't even with her. And the dog wasn't bulletproof, even though it had seemed as though he'd been fireproof the night he'd saved her.

The sounds of boxes overturning erupted from the shadows in the alley next to the store. Tracy took off, running to her car. She'd rather the attacker just come out in the light so she could face off with him. But what she really wanted was to not face him at all.

Terror coursed through her.

Her car was only a few feet farther but might as well have been a mile away.

She looked back and saw a shadowy figure standing in the alleyway. Jay's attacker? She couldn't be sure. But she was nearly certain she saw the glint of a knife in his hand. When he saw her, he started running toward her. Tracy put on an extra burst of speed and hoped it would be enough.

Car lights shone from another direction, closing in on her. The attacker's accomplice? Was he going to run her down?

Her heart in her throat, she heard the vehicle screech to a halt behind her and someone exit just as she reached her car door. She wouldn't have time to unlock it. Not with her hands full of groceries. Not with her hands shaking. She dropped the bags.

And now he was breathing down her neck. She thought

she heard him say something, but her heart was beating too loudly for her to make out the words.

Tracy whirled to face her enemy and squeezed the button on the pepper spray.

Pain erupted in and around his eyes, which he squeezed shut reflexively. David coughed profusely, backing away from Tracy and into his truck. He couldn't see where he was going, but he had to get fresh air. He blinked a hundred times, despite the pain, as his eyes filled with tears, the body's natural defensive response—all while Tracy apologized profusely.

Coughing to clear his lungs, he held his hand out for her to keep her distance, though he didn't know why. He just wanted her to back off.

He bent over his knees, coughing again, blinking some more. He wouldn't be driving home anytime soon.

Then Tracy grabbed his arm. "I'm so sorry, David. I thought…I thought…"

"Just give me a minute," he said, sounding gruffer than he'd like. But he couldn't help it.

Next to his truck, David dropped to the ground and sat there, leaning his head back against the tire.

"What can I do to help?" she asked. "Please tell me. Let me take you to the ER. They can give you something to flush out the pepper spray."

"No." He would be the laughingstock of this town if anyone found out what had happened.

"Oh, David, at least say you'll let me drive you home, then. I owe you that much. And we probably shouldn't stay out here."

Blinking a few more times, David got up. Coughing, he cleared his throat. "I'd appreciate that, because I can't see enough to drive myself. And you're right that we

shouldn't stay out here. But please stop apologizing. This
was all my fault. I should never have rushed up behind
you like that. But, Tracy—" David wished he could look
her in the eyes "—did you see what I saw? Was that why
you were running scared?"

He ignored the pain to listen intently to her reply.

She inhaled a long breath. "W-what did you see?" she
stammered.

"I saw you first, sprinting toward your car. When I
pulled into the parking lot to see if you were okay, I
thought I saw a man running toward you. But when he
saw me, he took off for the alley."

When she didn't respond he imagined her frowning,
contemplating how to answer. David reached for her,
found her shoulders and squeezed. He hoped he was
wrong—that there hadn't really been a man trying to
attack her—because they were vulnerable out here, and
he wasn't able to see what he was doing if the man came
back.

"I…I only caught a glimpse. Not even enough to give
a good description to the police. When he caught sight of
me, I just freaked out and ran. And the rest…you already
know. But why didn't you call out to me?"

"I did, Tracy. I saw you were upset and I was trying
to reach you to make sure you were all right."

"Well, all I can say is at least it was pepper spray instead of a gun."

David huffed a laugh. That was for sure. Still, Tracy
needed protection, and he'd try to talk her into getting
that weapon. Teach her how to shoot. He'd try to protect
her, watch over her, but he couldn't do that 24/7. Maybe
he could talk to the police and see what was going on. If
the man was following her closely enough to know when

to attack her in the parking lot, then she needed someone to keep an eye on her and make sure she stayed safe.

"Why don't you park my truck and shut it off. Lock up and grab the keys. Then you can drive me back to my apartment."

Heidi always teased him about his bachelor pad—the place he'd lived for ten years since his wife's death. There hadn't been a house to go back to anyway after the fire.

He tried as best he could to help Tracy retrieve the groceries she'd dropped, but he was more trouble than he was help. Once he was seated in the passenger seat of her Corolla, he leaned his head back, keeping his eyes shut. When she steered from the parking lot, David gave her the address. She headed toward town and he felt guilty that she had to drive him then drive herself all the way back home.

"Listen, maybe I should call Cade to escort you home. I don't like you driving back to the cottage this late at night, after that creep tried to come after you in the parking lot. Until they catch this guy, you aren't safe. I know what you said about not wanting to give up your life here, but you should go into WITSEC. Change your name. Get out of town. Something. Have you even told the police since we talked last night?"

"Look, I already have a guard dog. I don't need a personal guard. We've been over this."

Yeah, they had—and he still wasn't satisfied with her answers. "If it's within my power to help, to do good, then that's what I have to do."

"You act like you have a choice," she said. "You don't get to insert yourself into my life without my permission."

Ouch. That hurt. Maybe she really didn't like him.

"That sounded harsh," she said, "and I don't mean to be, but someone has already forced me to change my life once, and I'm just overly sensitive about the thought of that happening again." She sighed.

David wasn't sure how to respond. Maybe he was coming on too strong, too controlling, in his simple effort to watch out for her. She hadn't asked for his help, in so many words. But David had felt her need for reassurance, for protection, for a friend—someone to talk to—last night in the cottage. And she'd shared her past with him. Something she hadn't shared with others in Mountain Cove, or so she'd said.

David sensed when Tracy turned right.

"Okay, this is Main Street. Where to now?"

"Go all the way through town to Crescent then take a left. You'll see the complex on the right." David felt like more of an idiot by the minute. She didn't want him involving himself. "I'm sorry if I overstepped."

The thing was, David wasn't about to go away until this was over, regardless of what Tracy said.

"Look, David. It's not that. Not really. I don't want you to put yourself in danger for me, that's all."

"How about you let that be my choice."

When she didn't answer, he hoped she was at least thinking about it. David could tell when she turned into the parking lot of his apartment complex. "It's all the way down, then the first building on the left. I'm upstairs. Number 201."

She parked the car and turned it off. "I'll assist you up, but I won't be coming in. And I'm not going to let you call your brother and force him to come out here to follow me back. I'll be fine getting home, and Solomon will be with me once I'm there."

"But what if that really was Jay's attacker tonight? What if he really is someone from Santino's gang after you? Seriously, you could have been in real danger. If you're going to go somewhere alone, take Solomon with you. I know what I said about him, but he's better than nothing."

David got out of the vehicle and Tracy assisted him up the stairs. He allowed it, wanting to keep her by his side longer, or at least until he figured out how to persuade her that she needed to leave town. Do something besides wait in that poorly protected cottage.

Once they were at his door, he turned to face her. He blinked hard and could see her better now.

"Your eyes are swollen. I wouldn't look in the mirror tonight if I were you." A teasing grin sneaked into her frown.

"I have some milk. I think that's supposed to wash away the pepper spray as opposed to water."

"I would offer to help, since I did this to you, but I don't think you need me."

No, David didn't need her help for this, and even though he wanted to keep her safe, he wasn't quite ready to invite her into his life. Besides, she'd spent the better part of the ride over rejecting him, putting him in his place.

David dug in his pocket for his apartment key and fumbled with the keyhole.

She laughed softly. "Here, let me."

After she unlocked and opened the door for him, she followed him inside. "You know what? Maybe you do need some help. I'll get the milk." She led him to the sink.

David could probably do this himself, though he might have to feel his way and stumble around. Still, he couldn't turn Tracy's offer down. After he washed his face and eyes with the milk, the burning sensation diminished, but he knew he must look a wreck. He eased onto the sofa of his sparsely decorated apartment.

His sister had tried to help brighten the place up, but

he didn't want a woman's touch. It brought back too many memories.

Tracy watched him from the kitchen. "Are you going to be okay now?"

"No, because now you have to drive home down that lonely road that curves through the mountains to the B and B, and that's all my fault. If I hadn't spooked you into spraying me, I could have followed you home." David blew out a breath and reached for the phone next to the sofa. "I'm calling Cade to drive you back." He should have called Cade to pick him up at the store, but he hadn't been about to turn Tracy's offer of help away.

She snatched the phone from him. "You're overstepping again. Sure, I got scared tonight and ran to my car, but the guy didn't get anywhere near me. And if he had, he would be the one with the face full of pepper spray. I'm fine, David. Marshal Hanes, Jennifer, said she would speak to the Mountain Cove police, and I gave her time to do that. I'll talk to them tomorrow, tell them what happened tonight, but they're already looking for Jay's attacker. You know that. I'm done running and hiding."

"Yeah, what I saw tonight convinced me of that." He pursed his lips, wishing he could retract the words.

"I need you to stop worrying about me. Just…leave me alone."

Then she left his apartment.

Wow.

That was downright cantankerous, to use one of his grandmother's words.

He couldn't remember anyone ever being so adamant that he stay away, and it cut through his pride. He hadn't realized he had such a big ego, but he wasn't used to having a woman reject him for any reason. It was always David Warren who did the rejecting. There hadn't been anyone since his wife, Natalie. No one had ever caught his attention.

That was, until Tracy Murray. Why her? Especially since she clearly didn't want him around. But there was something in her adamancy that made David believe it went much deeper and had nothing at all to do with disliking David.

He couldn't get out of his head the way she felt in his arms. There was more to his comfort and reassurance, more between them. An attraction; a connection that was dangerous to his well-being. So what was really going on? Why didn't Tracy want his help?

Regardless, he wouldn't stalk the woman.

Somehow he'd find a way to help a woman in need. That was all this was about; David helping to keep a woman safe—a woman who had a dangerous man after her.

SIX

Tracy exited the small but modern building at the edge of downtown that housed the Mountain Cove Police Department. She shouldn't worry too much about coming to harm in the middle of the day in front of the police department building, but she couldn't help but search her surroundings, glancing at every vehicle, every person who approached her. Or who walked across the street from her.

She hadn't gotten any sleep last night for jumping at every sound. Or the night before. The way Solomon watched her, as if he wished she would go to sleep so he could, too, settled her enough that she'd at least closed her eyes. But sleep had not come.

That was, until early morning, when she was too exhausted to care if her past had caught up with her. Except she'd had to get up and go to work at the B and B, cooking and serving breakfast. And then she'd cleaned the bedrooms. Jewel had given her the rest of the day off to take care of "this killer business" after Tracy had told her everything. Tracy had taken comfort in Jewel's concern for her safety that she'd heard in her friend's tone. Seen in her expression.

Throwing her bag over her shoulder, Tracy walked away from the building and headed down the sidewalk to her car, tension knotting her shoulders. She'd had to sit there waiting to see Colin Winters, the Mountain Cove police chief, for more than an hour, which had made no sense. Talking to her should have been his priority. The police didn't seem to have a lot of opportunities to fight crime in this town, and the one big thing everyone was talking about was the fallen hiker. Oddly enough, the police weren't calling it an attempted murder. According to Chief Winters, they didn't want to incite panic by saying there was a would-be killer on the loose.

Tracy figured they should worry more about protecting the citizens of Mountain Cove, warning them so they could be on the lookout for a man with a specific tattoo, than about inciting a panic. Good grief.

She'd said as much, too. But he'd assured her that when they had verified the facts based on the information Jay and Tracy had given them, along with what Chief Winters had learned from Marshal Hanes, then he would decide what action to take for public safety.

In the meantime, they were conducting an investigation.

He'd said the words with all seriousness, but then proceeded to tell her that the kind of violent gang member Tracy described when she shared some of her past couldn't hide for long in Mountain Cove. He would be found out sooner, rather than later.

"The good folks of Mountain Cove will push him up and out of here like the body pushes a splinter out," he'd said.

Tracy wanted to tell him that might be true, but the splinter could fester. There could be swelling and irritation and even infection before it was expelled. Who knew how much damage one of Santino's men could do before he was caught?

In front of her vehicle, she stepped off the sidewalk and kicked the tire, then slung her homemade blue-jean bag onto the hood, glad she'd bought a junker car so she wouldn't feel guilty for using it to vent her bad mood. She unlocked the door the old-fashioned way—with a key instead of a fob. Before she grabbed her bag off the hood her cell went off.

Maybe it was Jennifer calling again to give her some good news.

David Warren.

Tracy sighed. She still felt so bad for her last words. *Just...leave me alone.* And then she'd walked out.

He was only trying to help and any sane person would have accepted the offer. But David didn't fully understand what he was getting himself into. And Tracy couldn't risk his life by bringing him into her dangerous world. Besides, she liked him too much, and she sensed that he liked her, too.

For the best part of the two years she'd lived in Mountain Cove, he and Tracy had steered clear of each other, or so it had seemed, each having their own reasons. Now that they'd spent more than a few minutes together alone, Tracy knew there was something more between them, just under the skin. Maybe David hadn't realized that yet, but a woman knew these things.

Tracy was in no place to go down that road with him now. If ever.

But she knew instinctively that if she ignored his call, he'd just drive out to see her and make sure she was okay. She had to answer the phone—but she silently resolved to keep it brief and to discourage him from putting himself out any further on her account. She answered, forcing a smile into her tone.

"Hey, David."

"Hey." An awkward pause hung between them.

"I'm so sorry about what I did last night." What was she doing? He hadn't called her so that she could tell him she was sorry again, had he? Regardless, the words needed saying.

"Which part? You mean the pepper spray? Or the complete and utter rejection of my help?"

David's question left her searching for words. Frowning, she leaned against her car, watching the hustle and bustle of Mountain Cove, enjoying its small-town charm. Yeah, this was home. Nobody was going to run her off this time.

He huffed a laugh. "Listen, I shouldn't have said that. Besides, I blame myself for getting sprayed. And…can we keep that just between us?"

Her turn to laugh. She stared down at her secondhand boots, the scuffs visible just beneath the hem of her jeans. "Sure. It'll be our little secret. I wouldn't want the whole town afraid to approach me."

"Maybe not the whole town but…"

He hadn't said "Santino" or "Jay's attacker," but she knew that was what he was thinking. "And I'm sorry about all of it, if that makes a difference. I deserved the words." But this conversation with him was taking too long, going too deep, getting too personal. She could feel the pull between them over the cell phone.

"Why did you call?"

She wished she could tell him she wanted his help, but she had a feeling that once she'd said yes to that one offer of help last night, he'd glue himself to her side until her stalker was caught. David Warren had "fierce protector" written all over him. He might think he could protect her.

But it would never work.

What would he do, sit on her porch all night? Follow her around? He would die if he tried to protect her. She already knew from experience.

"It's Jay," he said.

She sucked in a breath. "What's happened?"

"Nothing happened. He's doing well, considering his injuries. He wants to talk to us both at the hospital."

What could that be about? "When?"

"Whenever we can get there. Where are you now? I can come get you."

Tracy eyed the police building. "No, I'll meet you at the hospital."

"Um, Tracy. You do realize he's in Juneau, right?"

She released a pent-up breath. "I didn't even think about that."

"His injuries were too severe, so they had to transport him to a regional hospital. Juneau was it."

Tracy was surprised he hadn't gone on to Seattle, but he'd probably needed the quickest care he could get. "What did you have in mind, then?"

"We can take a floatplane to Juneau together. I have a bush-pilot friend, Billy, who can be ready in an hour. I can come get you and we can grab a bite before then."

Oh, David was good. Really good. She smiled to herself. "I'll meet you at the floatplane dock in an hour."

"See you there." Disappointment cut across the line before he ended the call.

She'd just successfully rejected David again. She was getting far too good at this. What would it hurt to eat with him? Her stomach rumbled and she called him right back, but the call went to voice mail. Just as well.

On the flight from Mountain Cove to Juneau, David listened to Billy fill the time and otherwise silent flight with small talk about his adventures in the bush. At first David had wanted to focus on Tracy and get her to talk, but he realized that Billy offered Tracy a much-needed reprieve from thinking about her problems. A person could

carry around that kind of burden for only so long. And
she seemed to be listening intently to Billy's stories. Of
course, she was sitting next to the pilot, so it wasn't as if
she had much choice.

For his part, David only half listened. Sure, he laughed
and smiled at the appropriate moments, but he wasn't
giving Billy his full attention. They were friends. Billy
would understand. David scratched his head and watched
out the window as the seaplane flew over one of the many
channels of the Inside Passage, the Tongass National Forest and the mountains—always an awe-inspiring sight.

But the beauty couldn't drag his thoughts from the
seriousness of Tracy's situation. If what Tracy had said
was true and Santino or one of his gang members was
after her, then why hurt Jay and not Tracy? There could
be only one reason for that and it fell in line with Tracy's
fears that anyone involved with her would be in danger.
In Jay's case, he'd been at the wrong place at the wrong
time. But her explanation for rejecting David's help, that
she didn't want to see David get hurt, made more sense.
David was glad he understood. But understanding didn't
mean he agreed. He was willing to face some danger to
himself if it meant keeping Tracy safe.

David wanted to know what had happened, what Tracy
had witnessed to put Santino away. But he wouldn't push
her. It was enough that she was with him on the plane
to see Jay.

They arrived at Juneau International Airport and caught
a cab to the hospital. Unsure of what they would see when
they walked into Jay's hospital room, David led the way,
giving a light rap on the door as he pushed it open. He'd
already called Jay to let him know they had arrived in Juneau and were on their way.

The guy's face looked as though it had been used as a

punching bag. His left leg was in a cast and traction, his arms were in casts, and he wore a neck and back brace. He cracked a smile when he saw David and Tracy. Yeah. He was a trouper.

David watched Tracy's reaction and noticed she paled, though she kept her smile in place. "Oh…Jay." Compassion filled her voice. "I'm so sorry this happened to you."

"Don't be. It's not your fault." Jay had no idea what he was saying, but David hoped Tracy would hold it together. "The good news is I'm alive. After a fall like that, I should have died. But I have nothing more than broken bones."

"You look good," David teased. Somehow he knew Jay would take it in the right spirit. "What's broken?" Though he could see plenty.

Jay's chuckle was good-natured. "Nine fractures in my arms and legs. Broken ribs." Jay blinked his eyes. Even that looked painful. "Thanks for coming." His voice sounded weaker than it had on the phone. They couldn't stay too long; he needed to rest.

David noticed Jay studying Tracy. Her face still pale, she moved to the side of the bed. David had a feeling she would have taken Jay's hand—much as she had on the side of the mountain—but due to the casts there wasn't much of his hands exposed. How had either of them been able to hold his hand on the mountain without causing more pain? Maybe Jay had been in *that* much shock.

Man. David gave a subtle shake of his head, thanking God that Solomon had found the man and praying for his eventual full recovery.

His mind went back to that moment when Tracy had leaned closer to Jay to listen. Then she'd freaked out. He understood the reason for her reaction now and wondered if Jay's request to see them again had to do with the man who had tried to kill him.

"Thanks for coming," Jay said. "I wanted to thank the two people who saved me. If you hadn't found me I would have died on the mountain."

"There's no need to thanks us." Tracy glanced at David for his agreement.

He nodded. "No, the real hero isn't here. We knew the hospital wouldn't let Solomon, Tracy's search-and-rescue golden retriever, come inside, so we left him at home."

Jay coughed a laugh. "Is that right? Well, maybe after I get out of here, I'll meet Solomon. Tell him thanks for me, Tracy."

"I will." She looked to David as if unsure what to do or say next. "We should probably go now and let you rest."

"No." Jay blinked at her. Studied her. What was the man thinking? "I asked you here for a reason. I need to know that you believe me, Tracy."

"What…what are you talking about?" She edged closer.

"You believe me about the man who pushed me over."

"Of course I believe you. Why would you ask? What's going on?"

"The police questioned me. They say they haven't found anyone who fits that description. But when I told you about the tattoo, you had a strong reaction—like you'd seen it before. So I'm hoping you believe me and you can help me make sure they get this guy."

"Yes, I reacted the way I did because I've seen that tattoo before."

She stopped and appeared uncertain if telling Jay everything would benefit him or if he'd be better off not knowing. David wasn't sure about that himself.

Walking around the bed to where she stood, he placed his hand on her shoulder, hoping to reassure her, and then he addressed Jay. "Can I ask if there's any reason the police would doubt you, besides the one they've given?"

Jay grimaced, releasing a painful sigh. David wondered if that was from his physical pain or something else.

"Two years ago I tried to commit suicide," he said.

Ah. That made sense, then. They thought this was another attempt, or at least were considering the possibility. Except why would Jay make up a story like that? And how could he have described the Santino gang tattoo so accurately if he hadn't seen it? David didn't think the police would discount the tattoo or Tracy's history with the gang. He had the highest respect for the police officers he knew, and he wasn't sure why Winters wasn't acting quickly on this. Then again, he could see where the hesitation came from.

But what about Tracy's history with this gang? Was Winters seriously going to discount that?

"I'm sorry to hear that." Tracy placed her hand gently on the cast encasing Jay's arm. "I want you to know that I believe you. I talked to the police this morning and told them how I know about the tattoo. I think they'll believe you now, too, if they didn't before. I had a bad experience with members of a gang. That tattoo symbolizes their membership. I'll do everything I can to make sure this guy is caught. Now, do you believe *me*?"

"Yes." Jay blew out a ragged breath. "It's hard being stuck here. A friend came with me to see this part of Alaska. It had been a childhood dream. We'd already been here a week when he had to go home a day early. I decided to stay. It's so beautiful here I didn't want to leave. I had just gotten my life back together, too, after my suicide attempt. Have a great job back in Texas and now I'm not sure I can even go back to work there when I'm finally recovered. My family is on their way to see me, but they can't stay here as long as it'll take for me to get stable enough to move." Jay closed his eyes.

"Let us know what we can do to help," David said. "I don't live in Juneau, but I have a lot of friends and family in the region, and I'll make sure they know you're here. We'll be your family while you're in Alaska. Whatever you need."

"Thank you."

David thought he might have heard tears in Jay's voice.

Tracy turned to him then, a soft smile edging into her lips. The look in her eyes stirred his heart, the intensity there surprising him.

Not wanting to overtire Jay, they said goodbye and headed back to the seaplane dock.

"Your chariot awaits," Billy said with a flourish, winking at Tracy.

"Seriously? You're flirting with her?" Jealousy stabbed through David. It wasn't his place to be jealous. He couldn't believe he'd scolded Billy in front of Tracy like that. Thankfully, Billy seemed to shrug it off, holding up his hands in a "no offense" gesture.

David didn't think Tracy had noticed his reaction or Billy's attention and, for that, he was grateful.

On the short flight back to Mountain Cove, David could feel the tension coming off her. In the short time he'd spent with her, he'd gotten to know her better and knew he couldn't push her to tell him what she was thinking. She didn't like to be controlled or manipulated.

David had decided to sit up front with Billy to let Tracy have some time to herself, as much as one could have in a small seaplane. He was the one to pay attention to Billy's stories and this time Tracy was the one who barely listened.

"Had a fire up north in the Kenai Peninsula again. They called in extra crews."

Billy'd had to bring that up.

David rubbed his jaw. "You know I don't do that anymore." Not since Natalie had died. If he had quit earlier, stopped traveling to fight the wildland fires, she'd still be alive today. He believed that to his bones. So he'd quit fighting wildland fires for the Forest Service and joined the Mountain Cove Fire Department, and he'd never seen a wildfire again. It had been too little, too late.

But he wouldn't go back to doing something he loved. The guilt wouldn't let him.

"I need your help." Tracy's words pulled David from his self-recriminations.

After her persistent rejection, David wasn't sure he believed her. But he wasn't about to turn down this opportunity. "Whatever I can do. Name it."

"We have to convince the police that there is a potential killer out there. I cannot believe any of this is happening. I need to find Jay's attacker myself. Draw him out."

That wasn't the kind of help he could give her. And he wouldn't even if he could. "I know you're frustrated, and I'll do whatever I can to help, but you have to let the police do their job. You don't need to go looking for trouble."

"If he's here, we have to find him before it's too late. Before someone else gets hurt." She stared out the window. "Because of me."

David couldn't help himself. He reached behind him and grabbed her hand. Held it. Squeezed. And Tracy didn't throw up her wall and pull away. "I know I already told you to go into WITSEC. It's not that I want you to go. Believe me, I don't. But maybe it's for the best."

"I can't leave now. I won't. But I didn't think I'd have to convince the police like this."

"Guys. You need to see this." Billy's voice called David's attention forward.

Smoke billowed in the distance.

"You don't think that could be a wildfire, do you?" Tracy asked.

"No."

David's pulse jumped and he pulled out his cell. He was assistant fire chief, but still worked shifts—twenty-four hours on, two days off—and should have been on today, but he'd taken it off to see Jay, so he shouldn't expect a call. But still, a text about what was going on would have been appreciated.

The fire crews responded to a couple of thousand incidents every year, most of which were EMS calls, and only a few were fires. House fires, apartment fires. Buildings in town. A few brush fires. No blazing wildfires like what they showed on the news in different regions of the country. The Tongass National Forest was a temperate rain forest and it was simply too wet here. The fires they did see usually involved the thick underbrush burning beneath the surface, smoking mostly. No tree crowns. So, no, this couldn't be a wildfire.

"Fly closer, Billy. Let's see what's burning."

David sent a text to his chief asking about the fire. When they got close enough to Mountain Cove, Billy circled around for a closer look.

"The grocery store. Oh, no!" Tracy sucked in a breath. "Veronica… She said she was working today. It's happening…"

"What's happening, Tracy? What are you talking about?"

She pressed her face into her palms. "It's happening all over again."

SEVEN

Tracy couldn't believe the devastation she saw as David parked his truck at the curb across the street from the grocery store to keep out of the way.

When Billy had landed the plane, Tracy had climbed into David's truck without even questioning what she was doing. Her car was parked at the dock, as well. But she knew as a firefighter, David would get into the middle of things, and she had to be there, too. Had to find out what had happened. If anyone had been injured.

If they had, Tracy would take it as proof that she had brought more trouble to Mountain Cove. And if that was the case, how could she live with herself? On the plane, David had demanded to know what she'd meant when she'd said it was happening again. So she'd told him about the fires Santino and his gang had started to target the people he viewed as his enemies, and the murders. Santino was a pyromaniac. But the details of her own personal trauma she'd kept to herself. The details of Derrick's death. It was too hard to talk about any of that.

David had listened, frown lines growing deeper. They hadn't left his face. Nor had he said much to her, but to be fair, he'd spent most of the time on the phone trying to reach someone for details. She didn't want this to be all about her, but she would still like to know what was going on. What he was thinking.

She climbed out of his truck and followed him across the street, sticking close; though she wasn't sure he even remembered she was there. Emergency vehicles had taken over the parking lot of the small grocery store. Fire crews had already put out the fire, and the acrid smell of recently doused flames lingered in the air.

An ambulance was parked there, too, its lights flashing, but there did not appear to be the usual urgency of emergency personnel rushing to save someone. That could mean one of two things. No one had been inside who needed medical attention. Or they were already dead. Dread soured in her stomach. She followed David past a fire truck and then he turned to face her. He seemed torn about what to say or do.

Tracy didn't know what to say, either, her own fear curdling with the hurt and pain of this loss in her stomach.

"Come on." He took her hand.

She thought he would lead her over to where some officers and firemen were talking. Instead he positioned her near a couple of cruisers, out of the way of the chaos.

"What are you doing?" she asked.

"I need to go, and you need to stay here."

"I want to go with you."

"It's not a good idea. Just let me find out what is going on—what happened. If this looks like arson or an accident. Find out if anyone was hurt." He grimaced and then his gaze pierced hers. "Trust me on this—you need to stay here. You should be safe. Plus, I can find you when I'm done. Okay?"

Tracy nodded. Her need to argue would only keep him from where he needed to be. She watched him trudge over to the authorities and hoped he could find out what she wanted to know, too. From here she could see what she hadn't been able to earlier: the store had been so damaged by the fire, it would likely have to be completely rebuilt.

There wasn't anything that could be salvaged.

Too many unbidden memories surged to life in her mind and heart, but Tracy didn't want to lose it here and now, in front of the onlookers across the street. She'd already done that in front of David twice now.

No more. She had to keep it together.

Across the street the crowd watched in dismay. Tracy scanned it for familiar faces and she saw a few but didn't know their names. Medics came around from the other side of one of the three fire trucks and into her view, heading for the ambulance with a body bag. And it wasn't empty.

Tracy rushed forward to meet them. "Who is it? Please, I need to know."

"Ma'am, step out of the way," one of the medics said.

A police officer grabbed her arm. "You shouldn't be here. Please leave the premises."

The burn of tears singed her eyes. "Who died?"

"Ma'am, we won't know anything until there's an investigation. Please cross the street and stand with the others or get in your vehicle and leave."

Oh, Lord, if it's possible, please let this be an accident. Please let this have nothing at all to do with me or with Santino's gang.

The officer assisted her to the edge of the parking lot, after which Tracy crossed the street and stood with the crowd. Some of them asked her questions. But she had no answers other than she knew that someone had died in the fire, though she kept that to herself. The community was small enough there was likely at least distant family or friends of the grocery store's employees or customers, whoever had died, in this crowd. Sharing that news wasn't Tracy's place, but surely they all had eyes and could see for themselves.

Finally she saw David emerge from around the charred walls of the building, shaking his head. The serious look on his face told her the fire had hit him as hard as if the attack had been personally aimed at him. Maybe all fires were personal to David since he was a firefighter. Or perhaps the fact that someone had died because of a fire put that odd mixture of anger and pain on his face.

She rubbed her arms, feeling those emotions herself. But what she couldn't know, and desperately wanted to find out, was if David blamed her.

Still watching David, she wanted to go to him, to cross the street and find out what he knew. He turned his attention from the burned-out shell of a grocery store to the emergency vehicles and then searched the parking lot.

He had to be looking for her. His eyes scanned the crowd and found her. He put his hands on his hips and she gave a little wave. When he started toward her, she decided that was her invitation, and after letting a couple of rubbernecking cars go by, Tracy crossed the street to meet David.

"You scared me half to death," he said. "I told you to stay put."

"A police officer told me differently and practically hauled me across the street himself."

Another frown from David. "Sorry about that."

Tracy didn't care. "Who was in the body bag?"

"Veronica was in the back of the store and succumbed to smoke inhalation. The fire didn't get her, but the smoke did."

The shaking moved from her knees up her body. She couldn't do this in front of everyone.

"Tracy, are you okay?"

"Of course not. Someone is dead." *Oh, God, please let it not be because of me. Because I'm in Mountain Cove. Please don't let this be a message to me.*

David ran both hands through his hair. What she saw in his eyes nearly did her in. He didn't even have to say it. Nausea swirled in her stomach and she bent over.

Hold it together. Hold it together. Veronica wasn't even family.

"What else can you tell me?" After everything she'd told him, he had to understand what she was asking.

"I don't have any answers for you. I don't know anything yet."

"But will the police believe me now?"

"If this was arson, I think Winters will have to listen now, speed up his investigation. Mountain Cove will have to be put on alert."

"Of course this was arson. What else could it be?"

"Tracy, you're jumping to conclusions. We don't know that yet." He gently squeezed her shoulder.

Even David didn't believe her. All Tracy wanted was to be alone. To process the fear and pain and sorrow by herself. But before she did, she needed to ask him the question burning inside.

"If it's arson, will you blame me? Because if I'd gone into WITSEC, then Veronica would still be alive."

David gripped her arms. He needed to make sure she heard him loud and clear. "Of course I won't blame you. You shouldn't blame yourself, either. No matter how this happened, it isn't your fault. Nobody else blames you, either, Tracy. Or will blame you, that is, if it's arson that's related to this Santino guy."

When he knew she'd heard him, he released his grip.

He could see in her eyes she didn't believe him. But they needed to have this conversation elsewhere. He had a feeling that Winters would come for her now, to ask the questions he hadn't been willing to ask before. David didn't want her to answer him when she was in this frame of mind.

"Let's get you back to your car. I'll follow you home and you can move your stuff in with Jewel." He'd decided to take a more direct approach and insist she move out of the cottage. How could she disagree with him now? Maybe he was being presumptuous, but he couldn't imagine Jewel would have it any other way.

"I'll think about it. But this is Jewel's busy season. She might not have extra rooms."

If Tracy couldn't stay in the B and B with Jewel then she could stay with his grandmother. Both Cade and Heidi had gotten married and moved out of the family home, wanting a place of their own. David had even considered moving back in with his grandmother because he hated that she lived alone. Or was it more that he hated that *he* lived alone?

As he studied Tracy, she once again stirred that forbidden longing in him. He didn't want to live alone anymore. Except he couldn't afford those kinds of thoughts, especially when Tracy was in danger. Especially when there had already been an attempted murder and possibly an actual murder, if the fire was declared arson and Veronica's death was classified as a homicide. He was certain Chief Winters couldn't keep this to himself much longer.

David was ready to get her out of here and back to her vehicle. "Let's talk about it on the way."

When she didn't follow he reached for her, but she shrank away from his touch and looked at the charred remains of what had been the grocery store. "It's because I was there last night. Was with her. That's why he did this."

On second thought, David would drive her to the cottage. She didn't need to drive herself just yet.

She finally allowed him to usher her around the edge of the parking lot and away from the dispersing crowd. Finding his truck, he opened the door for her, and because she appeared so shaken, he assisted her up onto the running board and into the seat.

"I need to check on Solomon," she said. Her eyes were more blue than silver today and held his gaze. He could look at them for an eternity if ever given the chance.

In that moment he knew...

Nobody was going to get to Tracy.

They'd have to go through him first.

That sense of protectiveness burned inside him as never before, and he didn't know why. Even as someone who saved people on a regular basis, he had never felt this kind of sheer, blind determination.

What was it about this woman?

With the surge of emotion, David had the need to reach out and caress her cheek, to reassure her, to somehow convey the depth of his commitment to her well-being. He certainly didn't deserve her trust, but he wanted to let her know that he would protect her.

Something stirred deep inside—warm and unexpected, unwelcome and yet undeniable. He wanted to kiss her. Kiss the pain and hurt and fear away, if he could. And he had a feeling that kissing Tracy Murray could chase away his own pain, too.

Regardless, this was the wrong time and place. And not something David should even be thinking about.

Ever.

He didn't deserve it.

And the awful truth of it hit him—he hadn't protected his wife; he'd failed on that count. Who was he to think he could protect Tracy? But he had to try. He had no choice.

"My car is at the seaplane dock, which is pretty far from this side of town. Do you mind if we head to the cottage first?"

"Of course not." That was his thinking, too. He shut the door and marched around the front of his truck, trying to shove away his errant thoughts until only one thought remained.

Protect Tracy.

Inside his truck, he started the ignition and then left the grisly scene behind them. Instead of going down the street in front of the store that was clogged with traffic and onlookers from town, he headed down a back country road that was little more than an overgrown trail but would cut across and connect him with the road again closer to the Jewel of the Mountain.

David quietly stared at the road, listening as Tracy tried to hide that she was crying. It was something he'd learned to do with his wife—he'd known when she was crying without even looking. And he'd also known when to give his wife space. Or when he needed to speak up.

But this time he didn't have a clue. Of course, Tracy wasn't his wife. Far from it. But he knew that sometimes a woman just had to cry. David didn't want to interfere with Tracy's process. He had enough anger and hurt inside for the both of them.

Veronica Stemson was thirty-four and had gotten divorced a couple of years ago. He thought she might have been seeing someone. Her mother was still alive, but her father had passed five years ago. She had one sibling still in the area. Funny how he knew so much about her. Come to think of it, maybe Cade had dated her in high school.

That was what life was like in a small town—everyone was connected. A death like this was a huge loss for the community. A complete waste.

He squeezed the steering wheel until his knuckles grew white and then composed himself, if for no other reason than to keep it together while he was with Tracy. She had enough to deal with. Both of them lost in their grueling thoughts, silence hung between them, except for the noise his truck made as it bounded over the occasional pothole on the back road.

Because he knew how caring the community was, he didn't doubt that Jewel would let Tracy stay at the main house. She was considerate that way. He might have had a thing for Jewel, even though she was a few years older, if he hadn't met Natalie first and fallen madly in love with her.

If only he could let go of his own guilt for his wife's death and move on with his life. Then he would be free to love again. But David was a loyal man, loyal to his guilt, and he had no intention of letting go of that. No intention of falling in love again.

He steered down the bumpy excuse for a driveway past the B and B to the cottage out back. Yes, she definitely needed to leave this cottage, which was too far from the house for comfort, especially with a dangerous man out there somewhere. And now a possible arsonist. That was, if the fire truly was about someone from Tracy's past coming to Mountain Cove to seek revenge.

God, please let her be wrong about that.

They wouldn't know a thing until the fire marshal conducted his investigation. In the meantime, people could die. David needed to make sure that Tracy was safe and secure, tucked away in the main house before he could head back to find out more.

At least it was still daylight. It was nearing seven in the evening. The sun wouldn't even set for another two and a half hours and twilight lingered forever this time of year. Sometimes he thought the summer hours in Alaska were much too long. Sure, he could get a lot done, but it seemed the day would never end.

He'd barely parked when Tracy climbed out of his truck.

"Hey!" he called after her.

Her frantic rush to the cottage clued him in that something was wrong. And looking up ahead, he saw that the door was open.

David hopped out and ran after her, beating her to the door. "Just hold on," he said. "You can't just waltz in there. Let me check things out first. We should probably call the police." He wished Winters would get a grip on this investigation and finally decide Mountain Cove had a real situation going on.

"Solomon!" she called. "Come, Solomon!"

Dead silence was their only answer.

EIGHT

"Go ahead and call them. What are you going to tell them? Someone lost her dog?"

Cell to his ear, he frowned, then dropped the phone. "You're right. That's not going to work, and any explanation would take too long." David called the dog, too.

After hiking up to the B and B and asking Jewel if she'd seen Solomon, Tracy and David searched the surrounding area and called out using the command Solomon should have down by now. He wasn't perfect, but he was a good dog. He wouldn't have just run off like this, not when Tracy was gone. Besides, the door had been closed, securing him inside until she got home.

David called the dog, pressing deeper into the woods behind the cottage. He was here with her, after everything that had happened today. After the fire. She would have thought he'd want to be back at the fire station with the boys and in the middle of things to discuss the fire, and maybe even bring up a suspect to the police, if Chief Winters hadn't already thought of it. But she had to admit, she was comforted by the way he'd stayed by her side.

"Solomon, come on, boy," David called again. That he was here searching for Solomon with her kindled something in her heart.

One day she'd have to tell David about the night Solomon had saved her life. It would help explain what the dog meant to her, though she suspected he already knew.

And maybe David was beginning to mean a little too much to her, considering she wanted to share that with him.

She'd told him she didn't want or need his help. That had definitely been a mistake. When she'd seen the door to the cottage hanging open, she was more than glad David was here with her. What if someone had been inside waiting for her?

But if there had been someone there, David could have gotten hurt. If the burning today was part of Santino's retaliation—bringing back the terror he'd rained down before—then David or anyone near her was in danger. Something she already knew, but she hadn't realized how far that danger could reach.

"David, wait." Tracy rushed through the thick and lush forest of Sitka ash, maple, cedars and a host of other trees and undergrowth she couldn't name. A person could easily get lost.

He paused and turned to face her, pushing a leafy branch out of the way.

"Be careful, please. I don't want you to get hurt. What if *he's* out there? What if we run into him?" What if Solomon had caught his scent and gone chasing him?

He frowned. "Don't worry about me, Tracy. Stay close to me and let's find Solomon." Letting the huge leaf pop back up, he pushed on, and Tracy shoved through the greenery to keep up.

"I appreciate your help, I really do, and I'm not going to stop today until I find Solomon, but I want you to face the facts. You could be in danger, just by being with me.

Talking to me. Being my friend. Look what happened to Veronica."

"You don't know that fire was related to your situation." Hands on hips, David stopped again, searching the woods.

"Of course I do. And you do, too. What we need is for Chief Winters to see that, if he hasn't already. But if I've learned anything about that man, it's that he will get the facts before he makes any decisions. I can't actually blame him for that, though. Can you?"

"Not really. No. It's part of police procedure. And it takes time." David still studied the woods.

They'd gotten off topic. Tracy wanted to make it clear to David that being with her might cost him. Was she worth it to him? Either way, she couldn't ask him to pay that price. Nor could she *want* him to pay it.

David turned his forest green gaze on her, the lush vegetation behind and around him emphasizing the intensity in his eyes. Taking her hand, he squeezed. Reassurance? Her heart jumped. He'd encouraged her and much more. It was the "much more" that she was worried about. She should pull her hand away, but her heart refused to reject him again. This man was out here helping her find her dog. Inside, she smiled—helping her find Solomon was only a small thing, but sometimes the small things were what meant the most.

"Don't worry. We'll find him," he said with a wink and then flashed that grin she'd seen him use on other women around town. But now she knew it wasn't manipulation on his part. His charming smile was simply part of who David was. And he'd found a way to smile at her like that with all that was going on. After the fire that had them both on edge.

Reining in her thoughts, she focused on the task at

hand. "We should probably split up," she said. "You can call me on your cell if you find him."

"Are you crazy? We're sticking together."

She'd figured he would say that, but she was trying to be practical.

"So I take it this isn't a usual thing? Solomon doesn't usually run off?"

"No. Not like this. This isn't right." Tracy was afraid to voice her worst fear—that Solomon didn't run off on his own, but that someone had done something to him. Was she being paranoid? She felt alone in all this—except for David. Even the police were not taking any of this seriously. At least not yet.

"See, even Solomon isn't safe." Tracy paused, swatted at the mosquitoes and rubbed her arms against the chill as the woods grew darker. "Jay might be home with his family in Texas tonight, Veronica home with her family if I had gone into WITSEC. Oh, David, what have I done?"

David tugged her to him. Did he realize how he held her up, kept her from collapsing on her trembling legs? She hated that she'd shown him how weak she really was, been this vulnerable in front of him, and not just once. Finally he held her at arm's length and kept his gaze fixed on hers.

"I want you to listen to me," he said. "I know I urged you to get a new identity, so you could be safe, but you were right when you said you shouldn't run or hide. Anyone who could find you *here* could find you anywhere, even with a new name and identity. But this time we're one step ahead. We know someone is after you, and we'll be prepared. I don't intend to leave you until the police nab this guy."

His words bolstered her courage even as they made her realize she was crazy to think she could stand her ground—stay in Mountain Cove—without someone by her side. But she never would have pictured David in that role.

"Is that okay with you?"

"Oh, so *now* you're asking my permission?" She couldn't help but give him half a smile, even in the face of all that was wrong in the world. "It's too much to ask."

"You're not asking. I'm insisting."

"You always get your way?"

His smile slowly flattened. "Not always, no."

Tracy waited for him to say more.

David dropped his gaze. "I…"

"What is it? What were you going to say?"

"I failed someone before. I don't want to fail you, Tracy, but maybe…maybe you should count on more than me and more than the dog."

"Who should I count on, then? God?"

David's silence on the matter chilled her to the bone.

David wanted to reassure her and be there for her, but he reminded himself of his colossal failure that had come at the cost of a life. He'd said too much, and realized it when he saw the look of hope in her eyes.

David hadn't meant for her to believe in him—if that was what he'd seen flashing in her beautiful gaze. He'd only meant for her to know she wouldn't have to go through this alone. He definitely wasn't a hero—not like his father. Not like his siblings. And he wasn't sure that he was the person Tracy should count on. Of course, he believed in prayer and that God listened to his prayers. Answered them, too. But David couldn't reconcile why God would let him fail his wife. Why Natalie had died in a fire, instead of David, who'd spent his life fighting them. It made no sense.

Aware that Tracy waited for his reply, he searched for the answer to her question. Deep inside, he knew what it was, and despite his own struggles, he couldn't withhold it from her. "Of course you can count on God. So pray hard."

He sent a teasing grin her way to lighten the moment and started off again. "The sun's going to set before we find that dog of yours if we don't get busy. Dusk in the forest is dark."

He caught Tracy's frown; saw her shoulder sag a little. Since they hadn't found Solomon yet, he knew she had reason to be worried.

Even as they searched deeper in the woods David started to think this might be some sort of trap. Was the Santino gang member using the dog as bait to draw them away from safety? David was glad he carried a gun. As always, his weapon was tucked safely in the waistband holster clipped to his belt. Besides, he was equally concerned about coming across a bear as he was a two-legged killer.

Finally, after they'd searched long and hard, calling for the dog without receiving the hoped-for response, David pulled out his cell and prayed for a decent signal. To Tracy, he said, "I'm calling in the family. The more the merrier."

He didn't want to incite more fear than Tracy already carried, but he wanted reinforcements. This was taking much longer than it should. There could be no doubt that something was wrong. Something had happened to Solomon.

Before the call went through, he heard barking in the distance. Solomon? He gazed in the direction from which the sound came. A glance at his phone told him he'd lost the signal, so he tucked it away.

"It's faint, but it's Solomon!" Tracy took off as fast as she could make it through the undergrowth. Good thing she had on jeans, he thought absently. But he should lead the way in case this was a trap.

He caught up then pushed past her. He pressed his hand against the gun in his holster. "Listen, in case this is something more than your dog simply running off, let me go first. I have the means to protect us."

She frowned. "Don't shoot my dog."

"I'm an expert marksman, okay?"

He led the way, but at the edge of the trees he paused and put his hand out for Tracy to stop, too.

"What is it?"

David listened and his heart sank as memories of his childhood rushed back, confirming what he thought he heard.

"I think Solomon's barks are coming from there." He gestured ahead of them where the trees opened up to an adit—an entrance to what remained of an old mine— driven into the side of a mountain.

"What's that?"

"A shaft to an old gold mine. It's not a working operation, abandoned long ago. There's none of the buildings you might expect, though some of the area's old mines have been renewed in recent decades. Gold is what built the town of Mountain Cove, remember?" Or maybe she'd never known that to remember in the first place.

"I can't believe it's not boarded up."

"It was."

From the cover of the trees, David peered at the shaft. It looked as if someone had broken through the old boards put in place years before after it had been discovered that David and his friends had been exploring the mine. Probably, more should have been done to close it off for good.

"Let's go get him."

"Not that simple."

Tracy pushed past him out into the open.

"Wait! What are you doing?" David snatched her back. "This could be a trap."

"This isn't exactly the modus operandi of Santino's gang. Luring a dog into a mine?" She shook her head.

"No. Luring *you* into a mine."

"Like I said, this isn't the way they have worked in the past."

"Was pushing someone over a ledge something they've done before?"

Tracy's silence was answer enough.

Chambering a round into his gun, David led the way. If nothing else, they could disturb a bear. Either way, David was prepared. "Doesn't matter if it's their MO or not—we can't go in. It's not safe."

"Then how do we get Solomon out? Since he hasn't already come out on his own, something's wrong."

"Maybe he found someone who is injured inside the mine, just like he found Jay."

Except Solomon sounded different than he had that day on the trail. Uncertainty crawled over David. They stood at the yawning opening of the old mine, listening to Solomon's barks echo inside.

"I can't take this anymore." Tracy moved past David to enter the shaft, knocking a board over.

"No you don't." David grabbed her arm and held fast. "It's too dangerous."

Solomon yelped as if he was in pain.

David wasn't sure what to do. He couldn't let Solomon suffer. What had the dog gotten into? Had he found someone? Or worse, had someone taken the dog to lure Tracy inside? *Lord, what do I do?*

Tracy put her hands on her head. "We can't just leave

him down there, David. But how are we going to get him out? We don't even have flashlights."

"I don't know."

"Solomon! Come, boy, come," she called, desperation in her cries.

"All right. I used to play in this mine when I was a kid—that is, until Dad found out. After that, it was boarded up to prevent anyone from getting hurt, but obviously someone wanted inside."

"What are you saying?"

"I know my way, if memory serves me."

"Didn't you just tell me it's too dangerous? And…I can't let you do that for me."

Tracy stared up at the sky as if she could find a way to Solomon there. David figured it was more about hiding the raw emotions pouring from her face, but he had already seen and his heart twisted.

"Solomon… He saved my life." She lowered her gaze to meet his. "I have to do something to help him."

At the look in her eyes, David saw the depth of her devotion to the animal and it left him with more questions about what had happened that sent her into hiding in Mountain Cove.

"I know that he's important to you, but the mine itself is dangerous enough, even if there's no one lying in wait to attack you. Maybe this isn't how a Santino gang member would normally operate, but you can't be sure, and what if Jay's attacker took Solomon into the mine to draw you in? What if he just wants to get you alone? Think about it. On the trail, he wanted you alone, but that plan was foiled when Jay ran ahead of you. And last night at the grocery store, he was ready to attack before I drove up. Today's fire was only a warning."

"But I've been alone at the cottage all along."

David scratched his chin. Good point. "Except he obviously doesn't know you're staying there. Maybe if he's followed you at all, he's seen you drive up that way and thought you were staying at the actual main house. Maybe he didn't even know about the cottage." Except Solomon had been taken from the cottage. "That is, until now," he added.

David was jumping to a lot of conclusions. He wasn't a detective, but he cared about keeping Tracy safe. And he hadn't wanted to scare her, but maybe she needed to open her eyes.

He'd make some demands from Chief Winters as soon as he could. Find out what the police knew about what was going on and if they were actually searching for this guy. But in the meantime, Solomon was their main concern. And if the dog had found someone else, they'd deal with that, too.

There was nothing for it. He pulled his cell phone out, grateful for the signal, and called Cade. To Tracy, he said, "I need someone to know where we are, in case something happens."

Her eyes widened. "We're going in?"

He pursed his lips, then said, "We're going in."

Still, he didn't intend to go too far. Without flashlights they couldn't anyway. They would see what they could and get out. And then they'd know more about what was needed. Once the appropriate help arrived, bringing the right equipment, they would proceed with taking the proper precautions in extricating Solomon and whoever else they could retrieve.

But what else would they find? Another victim?

Or was the man who wanted to kill Tracy waiting for them inside the mine?

NINE

Tracy stayed right behind David as he crept into the opening of the mine.

This had "bad idea" written all over it, but for the life of her, Tracy didn't know what else to do. At least they could take a look.

David had called his brother Cade to let him know what was going on and had received a stern warning in reply as though David was a child instead of the eldest brother. But Cade didn't have to listen to Solomon's barks turn into whining pleas, the sound of which broke Tracy's heart.

She couldn't think with clarity.

And then his whines turned to a low growl… What was going on?

Could there be a bear down there?

Or maybe David was right—this was a ploy to lure them inside.

"We're just going until the light from the opening no longer guides us, right?" Tracy asked.

"Right."

God, please keep us safe. Please let us find Solomon, or let him come to us before we have to go too deep.

"And then what? Solomon sounds like he's much deeper in the mine than we can go."

"I don't know. I'm making this up as I go."

She wished he would have kept that to himself, though she sort of already knew. Anyway, this was her fault, not his. She'd talked him into something he didn't want to do. Something she didn't want him to do for her, but she'd had no choice. She'd needed his help.

"We're coming, Solomon. Just hold on," she called into the shaft. She wasn't sure if calling out to him was a good idea, but it was too late to worry about that now.

As they crept forward, darkness slowly swallowed them.

"Hold on to me," David said.

"Why?"

"Just in case. I don't want to lose you."

Tracy hesitated.

He sighed. "Don't worry. I won't bite."

"You *won't* bite not you *don't* bite? Are you saying that sometimes you do?"

"Maybe." His reply held laughter behind it; much-needed levity for the moment.

Though she barely saw it, she liked that he could elicit a small smile even during an intense situation such as this.

Unsure exactly how he wanted her to hold on to him, she pressed her hand against his shoulder and felt a zap of an electric current. She instantly snatched her hand back. Entirely inappropriate.

She'd already been in his arms and let him comfort her through her tears, but this was different.

Instead she wrapped a finger around his belt loop. Clinging to safety at the moment was more important than her self-consciousness. And David Warren was the definition of *safety*.

"I'm sorry. I can't see much farther," he said. "This

isn't going to work. I should have known to grab a flashlight from my truck, but I didn't think we'd be attempting to navigate an old mine."

David turned around, and with Tracy's finger entangled in his belt loop, her arm wrapped around him so that she was pressed against him. That seemed to take him by surprise as much as it did her. Using his free hand, he grabbed her arm but didn't push it away. He held his gun in his other hand.

"Are you okay?" He was so close his warm peppermint-scented breath fanned her cheeks.

Her heart pounded in a way that had nothing at all to do with the desperate barks of her poor dog. No, she wasn't okay. She was entirely too close to David, feeling his sturdy form against hers.

"Sure. Let me just unravel my finger." She was glad for the dim light so he couldn't see the heat crawling up her neck and slapping her cheeks.

David turned away from her and Tracy was able to free her caught finger. Needing to put some space between them, she faced the opening of the mine and saw something.

Or someone.

Just a quick glimpse—but she knew she'd seen someone brush past the opening.

"Hello? Who's out there?"

"What is it? Did you see someone?" David walked toward the entrance.

Tracy trailed him. "I don't think it was your brother."

"I don't, either. No one could get here that fast." He paused. "Unless they were already here."

"Then stay here with me." Fear coiled around her neck. "Don't go out there."

A pebble fell from above. Then a few more trickled down with dirt.

"Watch out!" David pushed her deeper into the shaft and covered her body with his as the ceiling of dirt and rocks caved in.

David coughed in the settling dust, taking care not to crush Tracy but to protect her. He'd shoved her out of the collapse zone in the nick of time or else they'd both have been crushed under the tonnage. He should have paid more attention and looked for warning signs as he was trained to do when fighting fires. But when they'd entered the mine, he'd taken note of the rectangle timber supports lining the shaft to keep unstable rock in place and they'd looked to be intact and stable.

Had someone tampered with the lining?

Time enough to figure that out later. They'd survived, but now they faced another problem. Complete and utter darkness surrounded them. David needed an action plan. He'd been a complete idiot. For whatever reason, he couldn't think straight to save his life—or rather, save their lives and keep them safe—when he was around Tracy. And that didn't bode well for either of them.

David wished he could remain covering Tracy, protecting her, and that it would make a difference. But it wouldn't. He eased off carefully, dirt and pebbles falling away.

She hacked in the dust, as did he, until the air cleared enough they could breathe freely.

"Are you hurt?" he asked.

"No. How about you?"

He wished he could look her over to make sure that was true. "A few rocks to the back, but thankfully nothing big and deadly."

"What do we do now?" Her voice shook. "I can't see my hand in front of my face."

"The mine is deep, of course, but I'm not sure about the quality or quantity of our air supply."

Solomon's barking had subsided to only a few whines now and then. David's prognosis for their situation was not good. Somehow he had to turn this around. Increase their odds of surviving the mine. Or find a way out. He swallowed his fear. He didn't want Tracy to hear or sense his panic, adding to her own.

This should never have happened, and there was no one to blame but himself. But he could beat himself up later.

He grabbed her hand, glad for her strong and steady grip, and kept himself directionally oriented so he could find the wall. He placed her hand against the cold rock surface. "Here, stay right here. I'm going to edge over and start digging us out."

"Are you sure that's safe?"

"What other choice do we have?"

"We could wait for the others to get here."

"Can't waste any time. This could take a while. It's better if I get started." They needed light and fresh air. He didn't know if he could provide that for them, but he had to try.

"Then I can help you."

"No, please, don't move." One of them stumbling around in the dark was one too many.

"David, you can't dig us out on your own. I'm coming, too."

"Let me make sure it's safe, okay? Please. I need you to be out of harm's way in case I get in a predicament."

"As if we're not already in one of those."

"You know what I mean."

She coughed again. "Okay, okay. I'll stay here."

"Good. I don't want anything more to happen to you." David squeezed her hand and for some unknown reason pressed it against his chest so she could feel his beating heart. Why, he couldn't say. He wasn't exactly making sense to himself. Maybe he wanted her to know how deeply he cared, if something happened to him. And yet he continued to prove to himself just how much he didn't deserve another chance.

"Please, be careful." Her voice was soft, tender.

David closed his eyes, though in the dark it didn't matter, and prayed silently he could get her out of this.

"What do you think happened?" Her question broke the silence. "Do you think whoever we saw at the cave opening is responsible for trapping us in here like this?"

He swallowed the rising panic again. "I hope not."

But what else could it be? If this didn't convince Winters, David didn't know what would. He wasn't sure how the entrance had been destabilized, but Tracy definitely had someone after her. Was it connected to the man from her past who wanted payback? He didn't know.

He turned his focus to digging them out and hoped help would arrive on the other side soon. But would his brother think to be on the lookout for someone with nefarious intentions? Cade would try to call him in a few minutes, and when he didn't get a response, he'd come looking, though cell reception was iffy this far out of Mountain Cove. He hoped Cade wouldn't come alone. Now David wished he had gone into more detail when telling his brother about their search for Solomon.

God, please, let Cade bring reinforcements. Isaiah and Adam. Chief Winters would be a nice addition, too, except he would be all over David for entering the mine. He wasn't alone there.

David hit the wall of dirt and rock and felt his way to the top, figuring there might be an end to the pile, something he could dig his way through. Even if he made a small hole through to the other side, that would encourage him. And right now he definitely needed a boost.

He pressed his palms against the rubble to find traction and made sure it was solid. The last thing he needed was to create a rockslide that would bury him and take Tracy down, too.

"You okay back there?" he asked.

"I'm fine. What are you doing?"

"I'm climbing to the top of this pile and then I'll start digging, removing rocks and dirt. If this turns out to be a mistake and it slides, please back out of the way but don't lose contact with the wall. I can find you that way. Understand?"

"Yes." Tracy's voice was barely a whisper. "Please be careful, David."

"I will." *I promise.* The words zinged back to him from the past—the same words he'd said to his wife when he'd left for the Kenai Peninsula to fight a wildfire. He'd promised Natalie that he'd come back and he had, but she was dead before he got there.

David started up the pile of rubble, finding his way by feeling and gripping the larger boulders. He and Tracy were fortunate they hadn't been completely crushed. Regardless, he didn't know if he could forgive himself for making such a stupid mistake as coming in here without backup or proper equipment.

Again, he pulled his thoughts back to the task at hand.

He'd equate this experience to rock climbing with a blindfold. He wouldn't be surprised if there was already such a sport, something extreme-sports addicts participated in. He had about ten feet or so to climb, with only a few more to go. Tucking his foot against a secure boulder, he reached up and felt his way for his next hold.

Then everything shifted and collapsed beneath him. Somewhere in the chaos, Tracy's scream broke through.

TEN

Both hands against the wall and eyes squeezed shut, Tracy turned her face away, pressed her forehead down and against her shoulder, even as she flattened herself against the wall. Screaming, hoping and praying through the rockslide. Or had the ceiling caved in even more?

Her bottom lip trembled. *Oh, God. Oh, God. Oh, God... please help us! Keep David safe. Please, please...*

Before the dust settled, Tracy called out for him. "David, you okay?"

Nothing but silence answered. She was grateful he'd told her to cling to the wall because that was her only anchor. From deep within the mine, Solomon's intermittent whines broke through the trickle of pebbles, but she wasn't as concerned for him as for David. Now she realized what an idiot she'd been to pressure him into going inside—even a short distance—for her dog. They should have waited for help. Her stomach twisted at what she'd done.

She kept her eyes shut until she knew the air was clear so she wouldn't get dirt in her eyes. Though it didn't matter—she couldn't see anything anyway. "David, please answer me. Are you okay?"

Tracy opened her eyes, expecting to see pitch black.

But she could see the slightest outline of the wall. What was going on? Where was the light coming from? She felt her way forward, unable to see well enough to trust her eyes yet.

"David!" she called again.

When he still didn't answer, panic kicked in, her heart thudding against her ribs. She sucked in rapid breaths. *Lord, where is he? Please let him be okay.*

Then she saw a gap between the pile of rocks and what was left of the ceiling of the mine shaft—a hole that allowed light inside.

"David!" someone called from outside the entrance to the mine, the sound filtering through the small opening. It sounded like Cade. Relief whooshed through her that help had come.

"In here," Tracy cried. "We need help!"

He didn't respond, but she heard another voice outside. Heidi? Tracy tore her gaze from the hole and allowed her eyes to adjust to the darkness around her so that she could search for David.

"You guys, please hurry. David is hurt," she called, unsure if anyone could hear her.

And then she saw him. His body appeared lifeless.

Oh, Lord, please no...

Hot tears burned down her cheeks. Tracy dropped to her knees next to where David lay and assessed his injuries. No boulders or rocks had crushed him, and she thanked God that he wasn't pinned or buried.

But he must have hit his head. That was the only explanation for how he'd been knocked out. She wouldn't think the worst, but that he'd simply been knocked unconscious. As the clatter of digging erupted from the other side of the rocks and fallen earth, she edged closer to David and, with limited lighting and equipment, did her best to assess David's injuries. There didn't seem to be any broken bones. She ran her fingers gently through his dirt-filled hair, around his head, searching for a knot. There. She found it, along with sticky moisture.

Blood.

He'd hit his head. She prayed he would wake up soon with nothing more than a concussion, if that.

"You hear that, David? Help is on the way. They're digging us out of this. We're going to be fine. And you're going to be good as new. Thank you for protecting me, for pushing me out of the way. I didn't think I needed protecting." Tracy lowered her voice to a mere whisper. "But I needed your protection after all. Thank you for watching out for me, for being stubborn about my safety. You're a special man, David Warren. And I wish you weren't so good-looking."

Dirt and pebbles trickled from the top.

Her pulse jumped.

She hoped by digging her and David out, they wouldn't disturb the pile even more.

If there was a chance of another rockslide, she needed to move David. But first, Tracy did her best to carefully climb closer to the hole. She needed to let them know what was going on.

Anchored against the wall and a boulder wedged near the top, she called through the break in the debris. "Hello out there."

"Tracy? Is that you?" Cade asked.

"Yes. David's hurt. I'm scared that if you dig us out, the rocks will fall on him and crush him."

"There isn't time to come in any other way. This whole thing could collapse in on you both, Tracy. You'll have to move him."

"But I'm scared I'll hurt him."

"Did you assess his injuries?"

Tracy had some medical training, but she was far from any kind of certification. "I did, and I think he has a head injury." Man, she hated how the words sounded.

Cade's hesitation said volumes. "Okay, then. No back or neck injury that you can ascertain?"

Oh, God, why do I have to do this? Apprehension pressed against her chest. What if she made a mistake?

"Tracy, there's no time to waste, please…"

"I can't be sure. What if I'm wrong?"

"In order for me to climb through to check him myself, I have to move rocks, and that could put him in danger. I need your best assessment."

"No, I don't think he has a neck or back injury."

"Then do your best to gently move him away."

"But can't you call others to help? I've seen how they rescue people who get stuck in old mines or caves."

"That kind of expertise would take hours to get here, and we don't have time to wait. The shaft is unstable. We have to get you out *now*." Though he was patient, frustration edged into Cade's tone.

"Okay, okay. I'll let you know once I have him positioned out of the way. But be careful." Tracy hoped no one else would get hurt because she'd insisted on an ill-equipped rescue of Solomon.

She climbed back down to David and gently tugged him by the shoulders. Though she was strong, David was pure muscle weight and she struggled every inch of the way. Finally, after she'd managed to tug him several yards from the collapsed debris, she cradled his head in her lap.

"Everything okay, Tracy?" Cade again.

"Yes, David's at a safe distance, I hope." But as she

said the words, pebbles trickled from above her. "Please hurry!"

If this truly had been planned, the goal must have been for Tracy to be buried alive, and Santino would have exacted his revenge. As it was, this could still end badly, and in that case, he would have the pleasure of knowing he'd killed her along with someone she cared about deeply.

Someone she cared about deeply...

When had she started caring about David in that way that would lead to deeper feelings—feelings that were supposed to be reserved for that one special man? Especially when she'd made sure to guard against caring like that. Tracy needed to harden her heart, but right now she had to focus on getting David the help he needed. Getting them both out of this mine was far more important than issues of the heart.

"David, please wake up." She couldn't take this anymore. A knot grew in her throat. "Why is it that every time I care about someone, they get hurt?"

Saying the words out loud, she heard her own desperation. She couldn't let this happen again. She couldn't care about him. Tracy stiffened, her heart and mind warring with wanting to move away from him and wanting to hold on to him. She only wanted to protect him from further injury. But the urge to hold on to him was more than that. For far deeper reasons, she wanted to be close to him.

When she shifted to reposition his head so she could pull away, David's hand reached up, catching her wrist.

"Where do you think you're going?" David stared up at her, a half grin on his face.

She started. "You're okay. Thank You, God."

She tried to move away again.

He held fast to her wrist. "I asked you a question."

Even in the dim lighting, she could see a glimmer in his eyes.

He acted as though he'd been enjoying their proximity a little too much. Was he teasing her? But he'd been unconscious, hadn't he? Given their predicament, her pulse really shouldn't be racing at that look in his eyes.

"I need to find out what's taking so long." Tracy still held his head in her lap. Awkward. She eased away.

Was that disappointment in his eyes? Releasing her, David sat up slowly, gripping his head. He groaned.

"Just how long were you awake?" she asked.

"What?"

"I was…talking to you." She shoved thoughts of his reaction to her when he'd opened his eyes just now out of her mind. No point in dwelling on it. "Have you been awake and listening, just letting me…?"

"No. Not long. I heard a voice and I don't know… I wanted to wake up and find who it belonged to." His voice was husky. "And I found her."

Tracy couldn't breathe.

David winced. "My head is killing me."

"You're lucky you weren't killed."

When he pushed all the way to his feet, Tracy grabbed his arm to steady him. "Take it easy."

Had he forgotten where they were? What had happened?

Though he appeared disoriented, David found the wall, leaned against it and rubbed the back of his head. He'd found the knot. Then he gazed at her. "We *both* could have been killed."

Guilt washed over her.

Dirt and pebbles trickled from the wall of debris as Cade worked to clear a path. The ceiling shifted above them. David pulled her into his arms and shielded her against the wall, protecting her and trapping her at the same time. She was scared they were going to die. But there was no other place she'd rather die than in his arms.

She was in trouble.

A small rock tumbled. Scraping sounds coupled with more shifting and moving from the front of the mine caught David's attention.

Cade stuck his head through a hole he'd been widening at the top of the pile. "Okay, boys and girls. Sorry to interrupt your fun, but we need to get out of here."

He tossed a flashlight in.

"I couldn't agree more." David reined in his emotions and tried to ignore his pounding head. Tried to ignore the feel of Tracy's soft form in his arms.

She had power over him just as he'd feared that first moment he'd met her. It was the whole reason he'd intended to stay away from her. Even this dangerous situation hadn't prevented her effect on him. When Tracy had held David, spoken softly to him, he'd heard both her desperation and something more in her tone that had warmed him, drawn him out of his unconscious state. And he couldn't seem to shake this…whatever it was between them.

Nor could he be open with her about it, especially when he hadn't figured things out himself. He knew well enough he shouldn't connect with her on an emotional level, and here he was. It was too late. David slowly released her.

Dizziness swam over him.

She shifted under his arm, bolstering him. "I told you to take it easy."

Anyone else would have done the same thing, but it wouldn't have had the same effect on him as Tracy. He had to shake off these emotions.

"I'm all right." He untangled himself from her. He could stand on his own. "We need to get out of here."

"But what about Solomon?" Tracy's distress rushed over David.

From deeper in the mine, the dog's barks grew stronger and his form became visible as he emerged into the dim light from the opening of the mine shaft. Solomon nearly knocked Tracy over in his exuberance.

She hugged him to her, rubbing his head and body. "What happened to you, boy? Why'd you go so far into the mine?"

David should remind her that he'd likely been taken to lure them in. The trap would have worked perfectly if he hadn't called his brother to let him know where they'd gone.

Solomon started in on David then, jumping up to lick his face. He didn't want to push the dog away, but they needed to get out while they still had the chance. "Come on, Solomon. Let's get you out of this mine." He projected his voice toward their small exit. "Cade…"

"Yeah?" His brother stuck his head into view.

"A little help, please? Call the dog."

Cade called Solomon, pulling him up and out through the hole.

Then David assisted Tracy, positioning her as carefully as he could.

God, please keep things stable until we can make an escape.

Tracy climbed up ahead of him. The debris appeared to have settled and was packed enough that they could climb it without causing another shift. Once Tracy climbed through the opening, Cade and Heidi assisted her the rest of the way and David followed.

He was grateful that if this had to happen, it had happened during summer in Alaska. The sun wouldn't completely set until late, and even then, they could expect twilight until well after eleven. Not that he was afraid of the dark, but they weren't safe here and every bit of added visibility helped. "You guys came alone? You didn't bring Isaiah or Adam?"

"They were on their way," Cade said. "Terry, too. But I just texted them you're out."

"What happened in there?" Heidi rubbed her hand over the back of David's head.

He winced. It could take him days to get over this headache. He'd stop by the hospital and get his head checked out as soon as he could.

Heidi peered at him, concerned.

"We went into the mine after Solomon." David crouched down. "Solomon, come here, boy."

The dog wagged his tail and came willingly, then licked David all over his face again. Not something he'd normally prefer, but he allowed it for Tracy's benefit. When he looked up and saw her beaming at him, it was worth all the dog slobber in the world. But his chest tightened. He shouldn't be thinking along those lines.

She crouched next to him to pet her dog and wrestle him from David's face. "I think he likes you."

Cade and Heidi laughed.

"You think?" Heidi said.

"I'm sorry," Tracy said. This time she pulled Solomon off David, but she had to use so much force that she overbalanced and fell on her backside. Laughter erupted.

He liked her laugh and he liked her voice. A soft, compelling voice that had pulled him from an unconscious state. He couldn't seem to grab hold of her exact words— they hung at the edges of his mind, just out of reach—

but there'd been something inviting in them, that much he knew.

Then he noticed the thick marine rope around Solomon's neck. "This yours, Tracy?"

"No." She shook her head. "I don't tie him up. But someone must have tied him up in the mine, just as you said—to lure me inside. Solomon obviously chewed his way out. Good thing it wasn't a galvanized steel tie-out or he'd still be down there." She ran her hand over the dog's forehead and down his neck and back. "What would we have done if he hadn't escaped?"

Cade pulled out a pocketknife and cut the remains of the rope from Solomon's neck.

Tracy crouched to get in the dog's face. "What would I do without you, Solomon?"

She tugged him close.

"Tell me," Cade said.

David glanced around. "It's not safe to stay. We need to hike out of here. There's someone bent on harming Tracy."

"We don't have to hike far. My truck's just over there."

"You drove up here on these overgrown roads?"

"Yeah. I figured you'd done something stupid and I didn't want to waste time."

David wanted to glare at Cade. After all, David was his older brother and deserved some respect. He should be the one dishing out advice. Instead he tugged his brother to him. "Thanks, bro."

"You're welcome."

Together they hiked along the overrun trail toward the truck.

"So who is this guy, Tracy?" Cade asked. "Any ideas?"

"Someone connected to my past. You could all be in danger now because of me." Tracy sighed.

David eyed the woods. Tracy had caught a glimpse of someone just before the mine collapsed. Someone could be hiding in the trees. He put his hand on his weapon in his holster.

A twig snapped somewhere in the shadows of the forest.

Cade's truck was only fifty yards away, but it wasn't close enough. David shook off a wave of dizziness, retrieved his weapon from the holster and grabbed Tracy's hand. He picked up his pace. Cade and Heidi followed his lead. The person after Tracy—a killer, an arsonist from her past—could be watching them now. He shuddered to think what a person like that could do to the small town of Mountain Cove.

He feared Jay wouldn't be the last person attacked, that Veronica wouldn't be the last person to die. He feared in the end, he would fail Tracy.

ELEVEN

"I don't know if I can do this to you, Jewel." Tracy peeked between the curtains to see Cade and David talking to Terry, Cade's police friend, who stood next to his cruiser. "You need this room for your income. Bad enough I was taking up space in your cottage."

"There's nothing I wouldn't do for someone I care about."

Tracy pulled her gaze from the three men and looked at Jewel, who leaned, arms folded, against the doorjamb. In her midforties, Jewel was beautiful, with a quiet and elegant grace about her. Her ash-blond hair, long and straight, hung down past her shoulders. Tracy pictured her as the kind of woman who would wear it the same way even into her sixties and seventies and look just as beautiful.

Moving to Mountain Cove, Tracy had tried at first to avoid any close friendships, but Jewel had refused to be pushed away. "Thanks. I care about you, too. That's why I'm not sure this is a good idea. What if—?"

"You don't need to worry." Jewel closed the bedroom door and came all the way into the room. "The boys down there are going to switch out watching the house while the police track this guy down. We stick together here in Mountain Cove. Nobody is going to do this to one of our own."

"But he already did. His fire at the grocery store killed Veronica."

Jewel frowned and sat on the bed. It was covered with a gorgeous mariner quilt, and Jewel spread her hand over the design. "Veronica's grandmother quilted this. The woman lives in Massachusetts. She sent it to me a few years back. This along with two more in the other guest rooms. She stayed here once years ago when she came to visit Veronica."

How could Tracy ever make up for any of this? "It's my fault. She'd still be alive if it wasn't for me. And by letting me stay here, you're putting yourself in danger. And what about your guests?" Tracy rubbed her arms and stared at the window again. The woods surrounding the B and B made for a beautiful natural setting, but a killer could hide there and make a plan to attack them, undetected. "I should contact Jennifer, Marshal Hanes, and go into WITSEC. I shouldn't stay here for even one night."

Jewel was at her side and hugged her. Then she held her at arm's length. "Now, you listen to me. None of this is your fault. You didn't kill anyone. This guy who's after you is the guilty party. And he's just a man, nothing more. He's flesh and blood. My guess is that he's out of his element in Alaska. We'll get him before he takes someone else down."

"You can't promise that, Jewel."

"No, I can't. But there are no promises in life. People die every day, people who don't have a killer after them." Jewel released Tracy and adjusted the earth-colored drapes. "I lost my husband a few years back. He was a firefighter—he mentored David Warren, in fact. But he didn't die fighting a fire. No. He had to get struck by lightning when he was out hiking in the mountains. A lightning strike killed my husband."

"I'm so sorry," Tracy said.

"Do you hear me? Lightning killed him. We never get lightning here. He put his life at risk all the time for his work, and the thing that killed him was literally a bolt out of the blue. There are no guarantees. We have to live each moment as if it was our last. Treasure the time we're here. Cherish our loved ones. So if you don't want to run and hide, if you want to stay here with your friends, we'll stand with you in this."

The depth of Jewel's conviction touched a place equally as deep inside Tracy. How could she leave people who were that committed and loyal? And yet how could she stay?

"David thinks that if the guy could find you here, he could find you anywhere, even if you had a new identity," Jewel added.

Tracy wasn't as sure about that and wondered if David was only trying to justify a reason for Tracy to stay. That thought zinged through her—why would he care so much? She smiled inside. After the way he'd acted in the mine, she had no doubt as to the reasons. There was a strong pull between them, but Tracy knew better than to succumb to her attraction or any feeling she might have for him.

Plopping on the bed, she pressed her hands to her face. "I don't know about this."

Jewel lightly squeezed her shoulder. "You need to rest and then you'll see things more clearly. This is one of the rooms with a private bath. If you don't feel like joining us for dinner, I can bring up a tray."

"No, Jewel. I should help you serve. It's my job."

"Piffle. I'd say you need a day or two off. I have more than enough friends in town that can help when I need it."

The way Jewel eyed her, Tracy was reminded that she'd given Tracy a job because she'd felt sorry for her. She'd been her charity project—in the nicest possible way. Tracy hadn't come to town begging, but somehow Jewel had known she'd needed a refuge. She smiled at the woman.

"Thank you." The words creaked out. She could never fully express the debt of her gratitude.

Jewel gave her an easy, knowing smile then exited through the door, shutting it with a soft click. Tracy needed a shower or maybe a long, hot bath. They'd already brought most of her things up to the room—easy to do, since she didn't have much.

Solomon had been sleeping in the corner on a mat. He lifted his head and whined, but he didn't come to her for attention. Today's experience had worn him out. Tracy stole one more glance out the window. The men were still there talking, the deep grays of dusk dwindling behind the mountain silhouettes.

She was about to let the curtains drop when David glanced up at the window. He caught her watching and his gaze lingered. Was that smile suddenly lifting his lips for her, or something one of the other two men had said? Her heart skipped all the same. She was grateful they didn't seem to notice David's attention on the window. She let the curtains drop and sucked in oxygen. She really couldn't afford her reaction to that man.

David Warren.

Somehow this nightmare had given rise to him entangling himself with her, something that should never have happened. She would have been better off leaving town as soon as she'd heard Jay's story. But she didn't know where to go. Coming here in the first place, finding a place to stay and a job, had been a monumental task. She couldn't imagine moving again, and if she did, would

YOUR PARTICIPATION IS REQUESTED!

Dear Reader,

Since you are a lover of our books – we would like to get to know you!

Inside you will find a short Reader's Survey. Sharing your answers with us will help our editorial staff understand who you are and what activities you enjoy.

To thank you for your participation, we would like to send you 2 books and 2 gifts – **ABSOLUTELY FREE!**

Enjoy your gifts with our appreciation,

Pam Powers

SEE INSIDE FOR READER'S SURVEY

For Your Reading Pleasure...

We'll send you 2 books and 2 gifts
ABSOLUTELY FREE
just for completing our Reader's Survey!

she find a group of people who cared enough about her to stand with her, as Jewel had said? Would she find another protector like David?

Bone-tired, she headed for the bathroom and started filling the tub with hot water. In the bathroom, she noticed a cross-stitch on the wall. "Thy word is a lamp unto my feet, and a light unto my path. Psalm 119:105."

God, what do I do?

"You don't get to order my officers around." Chief Colin Winters worked his jaw back and forth.

David stood on the other side of the man's desk. When they'd started this conversation this morning, they'd both been sitting, but as tensions had escalated, both men had gotten to their feet. "Terry wasn't on duty last night. He chose to watch over the Jewel of the Mountain on his own time."

"In police property!"

Winters had already had words with Terry, and that was why David was in his office to face off with the police chief. "To let the killer know we're onto him. To scare him off."

"First off, we don't know there is a killer. Nobody's been murdered, that we know of. And even so, scare him off? We want to catch him, Warren."

"I thought we wanted to protect the town."

Chief Winters crossed his arms and eyed David. "You want to run the police department, then you can get a job and work your way up. You'll have to go through me every step of the way."

David ground his molars. "Why are we arguing? We both want the same thing. To catch this guy and protect the town. There's a killer out there, whether you know it yet or not. We know Tracy is in danger. Others, as well.

Why are you being so stubborn? Let's protect Tracy and catch this guy."

Winters relaxed his jaw.

David saw that as his chance to press the man. "I want to know what you've found in your investigation. Why is it taking so long?"

Maybe he shouldn't have made those demands or added that last part. He'd probably sent the man over the edge and would get kicked out of his office. But they'd known each other long enough that Winters respected David as much as David respected him, though tempers were too high to really demonstrate that respect right now.

To David's surprise, Winters dropped his arms and took a seat. He blew out a breath, obviously regaining his composure. "Sit down."

David did as he was asked and welcomed the chance at a civil conversation.

"I know what this is. I know what you're trying to do."

David stiffened, not liking where he suspected this was going.

"You're turning this into a way for you to make up for the past."

Was he that obvious to others? He hoped not. But his throat grew thick all the same. "What are you talking about?"

Tapping his fingers on his desk, Chief Winters studied him. "Never mind. Look, Warren, it *is* summer, and we've got lots of visitors coming through town with the cruises or to hunt and fish, using the cabins spread out in the woods and on the nearby islands. I'm in a precarious position here. I can't incite panic and scare all the tourists off until I have solid evidence. That said, there's only a couple of ways in and out of this town, and my department is on full alert. We're all looking for this guy who fits Jay's description. According to Tracy, this man might be after her, but she can't give a description."

"The tattoo. That's description enough. And there is no 'might' about it. Someone tried to get at her from the alley at the grocery store."

Winters arched a brow. David realized he might not have been informed of that incident. They hadn't called the police then.

"Then it burned down the next day." David knew they were still waiting to hear back from the fire marshal's investigation to find out if it was arson. "And then she saw someone at the mine last night before it collapsed."

Was Winters even listening?

"Again, circumstantial. Seeing someone there just before the collapse doesn't mean they caused it. Though I'll admit, it does look suspicious. We're investigating how it collapsed, and then we can tell you if it was intentional. But it could just as easily have been an accident. The mine was clearly marked as dangerous." He sent David an accusing look.

David had no response to that and shifted in his seat.

Winters deepened his frown. "By the way, how's your head?"

"It hurts, but I'll live."

"I hope you're not driving around town. You need to rest. That'll give you clarity, too, so you can be sure you're really thinking this through and not just reacting emotionally."

Frustration boiled in David's gut. "You know me better than that. And Tracy is not some paranoid woman."

"But do you admit she has a reason to be distrustful? Maybe even fixated on the idea that someone is trying to kill her?"

Standing again, David pressed his knuckles into the desk and leaned forward. "You go too far, Winters."

Winters held his palms up. "I don't blame her. If I'd lived through her experience in California, I would probably be looking over my shoulder, too. But I can't ask every person coming in and out of Mountain Cove to show their tattoos, and some of them have many."

"Then what *can* you do?"

"We can look for this man like we're doing, even though we don't have much to go on."

"And what about Tracy's protection? And Jewel and her guests?"

"I only have twelve officers, which isn't enough when the population explodes in the summer months. But... I'll concede on that point. Jewel and her guests at the B and B need a police presence if Tracy is staying there."

David wasn't 100 percent sure he liked the way Winters had worded that, as though Tracy wasn't his first concern. David had always trusted the man to do his job well before. But he couldn't help but think he was conceding because he had a thing for Jewel. Everyone knew that except Winters and Jewel.

"The Warren brothers will help you keep watch, then, too."

"No deadly use of force. Got it? Call the police if you see anything suspicious. And be careful. I understand how you think. You'd rather die trying to save someone than lose them, but the citizens of Mountain Cove don't want to lose *you*." Winters pinned him with his glare and David saw the truth in his eyes.

Satisfied that he was getting the police response he wanted, he said, "Then let's get this guy."

Winters stood and thrust out his hand. "You should

have applied to the police force instead of becoming a fireman."

David took Winters's strong grip and shook, feeling better about their conversation by the minute. "You're a good man, Colin."

Winters offered him an amused smile. "You had your doubts?"

"I knew you'd come through with some prodding."

David left the chief's office and exited the building.

Mountain Cove was small enough that most of the locals knew each other. Add to that the residents were made up of rugged men and women who could live through a harsh winter environment and who mostly packed weapons. Knew how to handle themselves. The threat came when someone was off their guard because they didn't know they were in danger. Someone like an innocent store clerk working at the grocery store.

But word had spread fast enough and people knew now to keep an eye out. He just hoped they didn't blame Tracy for Veronica's death. He hoped no one suggested she leave town. Most people he knew here would quickly come to her defense, but there was always one or two who stood apart.

What David had to do was figure out how to do his own job and keep Tracy safe at the same time. He had taken too much time off as it was.

David approached his truck, thinking back to the moment when it had arrived in Juneau. His shiny new truck had been meant to somehow fill that emptiness inside, and it had worked temporarily. Or at least he'd lied to himself that he was happy. Somehow when facing life and death, when trying to protect a woman he cared too deeply about, he wondered why he'd bothered spending the money on a new toy with all the bells and whistles, when there were plenty of other more important places to put his money. He already gave to plenty of charities and missionaries abroad. Local needs, as well. All more important and less selfish. But maybe he could give more and spend less on himself. He could have bought a used and older-model vehicle and it would have done the job. Still, as he climbed inside and ran his hand over the newness of the leather interior and started the ignition, he smiled. He was only human, after all, and though he hated his shallowness, he couldn't help but take joy in this small pleasure.

His cell rang and David dug it out of his pocket. It was the fire chief. They'd heard from the fire marshal. He'd determined the origin and cause of the fire. That had gone much quicker than David had expected.

"I'm on my way." David headed over to the burned-out hull of a grocery store. He'd already made up his mind—based on Tracy's reaction and what she'd told him—that this had been arson, though he hadn't wanted to admit that to Tracy. The fire marshal had sent debris to be analyzed for chemical accelerants, but ultimately it would be Winters's responsibility to investigate criminal activity if the fire marshal determined evidence of that.

Had he found something?

Or had David jumped to a lot of conclusions without any facts based on Tracy's story? What if he'd been wrong?

TWELVE

"Where is it?" Tracy grumbled to herself.

There wasn't anyone in the cottage to hear her complaining besides her. On her knees, she fumbled under the desk, searching for Jennifer's business card. It had been a couple of days since the grocery store burned down and the mine had collapsed, nearly killing her and David. And even two days since she'd seen David last. He had a job, after all, and had to work his twenty-four-hour shift at the fire station.

At least there hadn't been another fire in town.

For some crazy reason she'd almost started to believe he would never leave her side. She'd almost started to count on that when she knew good and well she shouldn't. And her heart ached a little, when it shouldn't. But between the Warren brothers and the police department standing guard at the B and B, Tracy was almost convinced she was safe.

And she was all the more confused. How long could they go on like this? Certainly not indefinitely. Tracy was trapped between someone who wanted to kill her and people who wanted to protect her, and she couldn't breathe. She needed to talk to Jennifer.

Behind her, Solomon barked, startling Tracy.

She bumped her head on the desk. "Ouch."

At least she recognized it as a friendly bark.

"What. Are. You. Doing?"

And the familiar masculine voice.

David.

Even the sound of his voice sent warm tingles through her. She crawled out of the confining space under the desk where the chair had been and rested on her knees. "I'm looking for something."

"You shouldn't be in the cottage. You shouldn't be alone. What's so important?"

"I'm not alone. Officer What's-His-Name is out there."

"No, he's not."

"What? He was sitting in his cruiser not five minutes ago."

His rugged face shifted into a deep scowl. "He must have gotten called away. Glad I showed up when I did."

"And you didn't pass him on your way in?" Tracy frowned. That meant that he'd been gone awhile and that Tracy had been here longer than she'd intended. Alone.

So much for having guard dogs of the human variety— they weren't reliable.

David held his hand out to her. Tracy took it and allowed him to assist her up. On her feet, she stood and realized she was in his personal space. Or he was in hers? Either way, his masculine scent wrapped around her and she took a step back.

Into the desk.

He was close. Much too close. And she'd missed him more than she wanted to admit. Her heart pounded, and unfortunately, her breathing gave her away.

The smallest of grins broke through his frown. Did he realize the effect he had on her? Not good. Still, he kept her pinned and stared down at her, his hands at his sides. "What am I going to do with you?"

Excuse me? You don't own me.

Tracy thought of a few more unpleasant retorts, but she calmed herself. David meant well. "I'm sorry. I can't find my cell phone anywhere. I think I lost it in the chaos in the mine. So I don't have my contact list or numbers. And now I can't find her card."

"Whose card?"

"Marshal Hanes."

"Don't tell me you're thinking of going into WITSEC."

Tracy slipped around him, putting space between them. He looked too good for his own good. Or rather, for Tracy's good. Tongue hanging out, Solomon lumbered toward David as if taking Tracy's place and wagged his tail. David reached down and rubbed the dog behind the ears.

"I'm not sure what to do." She needed some advice and had hoped that the marshal could give her that. She was still mulling over Jewel's words, as well.

If she thought he was going to try to talk her into staying, though, she was disappointed. David said nothing. Instead he studied her long and hard until she grew uncomfortable. She shouldn't care if David wanted her to stay or not. That shouldn't matter.

She finally averted her gaze. "So…um…I'm sure you didn't come here for idle chitchat." Oh, man. She could have said something much nicer.

It's good to see you. How are you doing? Something. Why couldn't she tell him that? Instead she sounded rude, and she hadn't meant it that way. She lifted her hand to reach out, squeeze his arm—she was far too demonstrative—and apologize for her tone.

"You're right. I didn't."

Tracy dropped her hand before making contact. So

much for good intentions. Not wanting to meet his eyes, she searched the cottage for anything else she might have left inside.

"We've finished investigating the grocery-store fire."

That got her attention. She jerked her eyes back to him. "And?"

"The fire marshal and Chief Winters agree that it was arson. To tell you the truth, I was hoping for something else. I was hoping that you were wrong."

Tracy sagged where she stood. "You were hoping I was delusional, that's what you hoped."

"No. Not that. But I'm having a hard time wrapping my mind around any of this. As I'm sure you are. You already told me about Santino and his gang and the fires. But is there anything, any details that would help us, that you left out?"

His question knocked the wind from her. Tracy reached for the sofa and made her way around, easing down into the soft cushion. Yes, there were details that she'd left out. She'd told him that she'd witnessed Santino burning a house, but she hadn't shared she'd been a target long before she'd been a witness. And she should tell him everything now, but she wasn't sure she could talk about it. Not yet.

David looked stricken at her reaction. "Maybe I shouldn't have asked you. Maybe I can get that information from the police if they're willing to share. I didn't think… I thought you'd be able to talk about it by now."

David approached her then sat on the edge of the sofa at the opposite end. Why did he keep getting closer to her?

"No, it's okay. It's just that when you asked me, I realized that I was running from that night in more ways than one. I wanted to forget everything that happened. I can't believe it followed me here. That he found me here."

"Then let's end this here and now. Let's catch this guy in Mountain Cove so he can never harm you again."

She shook her head. "Santino is still in jail. It's only one of his minions in his gang following his orders from inside prison. It will never end. There will always be the next guy until Santino moves on to another target."

"There has to be something we can do." David jumped up and paced the cottage, his presence and sturdy form once again making the cozy place seem much smaller.

"Santino would have to die first, and even then I don't know if his gang would stop targeting me. And that's why I can't know if staying here is the right thing to do. Jewel had a lot of brave words to say, and I'm privileged to know a community filled with such loyal people who have welcomed me as if I'm one of their own."

"But…"

"But I don't know, David." Tracy stood and blocked his path. She knew she should steer clear of him, but when he was this close, protectiveness and concern pouring off him, she couldn't help herself. She wanted to be near him.

In his arms.

Maybe she wanted him to convince her to stay in this hopeless situation. He made her think crazy thoughts, unreasonable thoughts. She shouldn't stay here.

Oh, God, please don't let him read my mind. Please don't let him see what has to be obvious.

But when he stopped and looked at her, his eyes were warm and soft, and she knew he'd done just that.

"I'm not usually so indecisive," she whispered.

He took one slow step forward and then another, forcing her breath to hitch again.

"I don't want to run again. I don't want to hide anymore. But I can't stay here knowing I'm putting everyone in danger."

David stood close again, and this time his hands didn't stay at his sides. He lifted his fingers and wrapped them in the tendril that had fallen into her face. She heard him swallow and understood he felt the attraction, too. But this thing with David that she couldn't let herself have went so much deeper than attraction. How had some gorgeous woman not snagged this man already? He was a prize worth fighting for.

She didn't want to leave Mountain Cove or the friends she'd made here, but David had quickly become her biggest reason to stay.

And he couldn't be.

"Then don't," he finally said. "Don't run and hide. Let your friends in Mountain Cove protect you, and at the same time the police can take this guy down, and then everyone will be safe. Including you."

Did David really believe what he was saying? "I don't think you truly know what you're up against."

He twirled her hair and stepped even closer. "Maybe not. But you're worth whatever the cost, Tracy. Don't go."

Then his lips made contact with hers and lingered, igniting something deep inside both her body and soul. Tracy breathed in the essence that was David and lost herself in his sweet, tender kiss that conveyed how much he cared, more than words ever could.

She didn't want this to end—this feeling of being cherished that David's simple kiss had ignited. But Tracy stepped away, breaking the spell. "I'm no good for you. I can't do this."

Anguish spread over his expression, regret in his eyes. "I'm sorry. I shouldn't have done that."

"Look, it's okay. I felt it, too. I kissed you back. But

this can't go anywhere, so maybe we should keep our distance."

"You're right. It can't go anywhere."

The look of complete resolution on his face wasn't what she'd expected, and for a brief, selfish second she wished she could take her own words back.

Tracy frowned and looked at the floor. It needed sweeping. "I should get back to help Jewel."

Solomon nudged her and whined, sensing it was time to go, too.

"I won't kiss you again, Tracy, but I'm going to stick around until I know you're safe, once and for all. I promise." David gestured to the door. "So if you're ready, I'll escort you back to the main house."

"Come on, Solomon."

Tracy walked with her dog and David strolled behind, keeping his distance.

When she caught a glimpse of him over her shoulder, she saw that he'd taken out his weapon and was scanning the woods edging the property. She didn't bother to protest. If she wasn't going to get a new identity—run and hide—then yes, she needed David's help. She needed his protection, but he brought his own brand of danger with him. He was a threat to her heart.

David watched Tracy hesitate at the back door to the main house. She glanced back at him but didn't smile or wave.

Fine with him.

Keeping their distance it was. As far as he was concerned, this was close enough.

Yeah, right.

He'd been a complete idiot to kiss her, but he'd been swept away by her crazy red hair and eyes with those flecks of silver on blue, and her soft-spoken personality, determined nature, courage—the list went on, including something innate he couldn't define. All of it drew him to her like nothing before. Well, since his wife. The thought of Tracy leaving, walking out of his life, had sent him over the edge.

Something about Tracy made it hard for the man in him to ignore.

But he had to try.

Careful not to scratch it, he leaned against his truck. So he'd start his shift watching the B and B and occupants a little early. He had two days before he was due back to the station. And then he'd worry about Tracy the whole twenty-four hours that he couldn't be with her or watch out for her as he'd just done. That had driven him absolutely insane. In fact, it had driven his firefighting buddies crazy, too. But at least they hadn't been called out to another fire started by this arsonist murderer. That was one positive in this whole mess.

Another was that he'd convinced Winters to participate in protecting her.

He'd parked at the edge of the property near the woods and mostly out of sight of the guests. He didn't want to scare them. He'd already tucked his gun into his holster and out of sight, as well, but that was more in keeping with Winters's request. David didn't have the authority of the law behind him, technically speaking.

Fortunately, Jewel had agreed to this setup and knew it was important to keep someone watching the place. And true to her word, she'd informed her guests of the situation, as well. He would have thought that news—that a killer was after one of her employees—would have scared her guests off, but that hadn't happened at all.

Jewel told him that an older man and his wife enjoying

their anniversary on a dream Alaska vacation had left the morning after Tracy moved in, but the other guests dug in deeper. Some had even tried to reserve another week, except Jewel was already booked for the summer. Were they hanging around to catch some action or watch the drama unfold? He thought it more likely they wanted their part in keeping Tracy safe. Though they hadn't known her for long, the guests interacted with Tracy every day and he could understand why they'd feel protective of her. David approved. Just as well to have the whole town, and then some, on guard and protecting Tracy since he was sure that he, himself, wouldn't be enough.

He shifted against his truck. This would be a long evening. He texted Cade to talk. Called Chief Winters to find out if they'd learned anything more. Jewel brought him some dinner—baked salmon in a puff pastry—and tried to coax him into the house at least to eat, but he refused, thinking Tracy wouldn't want to see him there after he'd crossed the line. Besides, he needed to watch from outside. Inside and near Tracy, and he would grow weak and stupid.

She was his kryptonite.

The symphony of insects harmonized around him, and though he'd plastered himself with repellent, the mosquitoes were relentless in accosting him. He especially hated the whining buzz in his ears. Dusk would descend soon enough and Terry should arrive around midnight, when it was finally dark, to watch over the B and B through the night.

David yawned, rubbed his neck and watched, waiting for the last light in the house to go out. Tracy's room. He knew because he'd seen her looking out the window that first night.

He fiddled with his cell, wanting to call her then remembering she'd lost her phone. Disappointment surged. He was like a stupid schoolboy who didn't know when to let go. But he had the urge to throw pebbles up to her window to see her open it and smile down.

Time crept slowly by and no one stepped from the woods to set the B and B on fire or attack Tracy, and for that he was grateful. On the other hand, if this guy was still out there, David would rather get the confrontation over with while everyone was still on full alert, rather than have the guy show up when they had let their guard down after too much time passed.

Finally car lights flashed in the long drive. David could tell it was the cruiser. The lights went off and out stepped Terry.

"Any news?" David asked.

Terry shook his head. "If he left town, he didn't leave by any of the usual routes, which leaves me to think he's still here."

David followed Terry's look to the darkened woods. "There are a lot of places someone could hide out there. He'd have to know how to survive in the Alaskan wilderness."

"If he knows what he's doing. Whether he does or he doesn't, don't worry. We'll get him."

"Hopefully before anyone else comes to harm." At the look Terry gave him, David wished he'd kept those words to himself. He almost sounded as if he thought the Mountain Cove PD wasn't doing its job. "I should get going."

Terry nodded his agreement.

David climbed into his truck, started it up and then rolled down the window. "Don't let the mosquitoes eat you alive."

He tossed Terry his bottle of repellent. The man scowled at David, but beneath his frown hid the hint of a smile.

Though David hated leaving, he'd grown tired and someone fresh would be better watching the house. If only he could have called Tracy just to say good-night before he left. He steered down the drive off the property and turned onto the main road. That was when he heard it.

That warbled sound that told him he had a flat tire. "Of all the…"

David pulled over to the side of the road and hopped out. Sure enough, his left back tire was flat. He must have hit something on the drive from Jewel's. He raked his hands through his hair, so not in the mood to change a tire. Not on the dark road in the middle of a short Alaska night when he was exhausted and emotionally drained and there was a murderer out there somewhere.

He got out the jack, lug wrench and retrieved the spare tire. After jacking up the truck, he glanced around and behind him. Pulling his gun out, he set it within easy reach, then bent over and started removing the lugs. He was on the last one when a footfall crunched, alerting him to someone behind him.

Before he could react, pain split his skull and everything went black.

THIRTEEN

David *had had the most exhausting week, deployed to a wildfire in the Kenai Peninsula. He'd been trained as a wildland firefighter, but 99 percent of the time, he was fighting fires away from home. He loved his job, but it was hard on his marriage and all he could think about was getting home to Natalie. Climbing into bed to lie on the best mattress in the world next to the best woman in the world. But as he steered his truck home in the early hours of morning, something didn't feel right. Warning signals pounded in his head.*

The smell of smoke filled the air and the fireman in him kicked into gear, stiffened and searched for the source. His phone alerted him to a text at the same moment he heard the blare of fire-truck sirens.

His house came into view, flames shooting out the windows and roof.

Oh, dear God, save her!

David wasn't sure how he made it into the house, but he hadn't waited on the trucks. All he could think about was Natalie.

He called her name. Shouted it. Kicked in the bed-room door but the room was already in flames... The heat singed him, burned his lungs. Without his equipment, he couldn't survive. And neither could she.

Strong arms pulled him out of his house. He'd wrestled on the gear he needed to go back inside, but it was too late.

And now she was gone forever. And he was alone.

The fire had caught him off guard—somehow he should have prevented it.

David coughed, smoke filling his lungs. Heat crawled all over him.

His eyes blinked open. Where was he?

He was inside his truck…and it was on fire. David tried the door handle, but it was too hot. He leaned back, pulled his knees to his chest and kicked the door. Again, again and again.

He was going to die. He deserved it. He should never have lost his wife to a fire. He should have seen the signs. Paid more attention.

But, no, he couldn't die. Not when Tracy was still in danger. He had to live to make sure she was safe.

God, help me!

"David!" Cade's shout penetrated the flames. Then the door popped open. Cade tossed in a wet blanket and David wrapped himself then jumped from the burning truck. Hitting the ground hard, he rolled.

A hacking cough overwhelmed him. Cade handed him water. "Let's get you to the hospital."

Anger at the situation coursed through David. "I'm fine. The fire truck will have what I need." Except his head was killing him, from the smoke inhalation and from the blow that had knocked him out. He wasn't sure he could take another hit in the head.

But at least he wasn't burned. He'd made it out in the nick of time. "How'd you find me?"

"I needed to get out of the house. Get some fresh air. Leah's crying. The baby's crying. And I'm doing everything wrong. I knew Terry was relieving you at midnight and I headed that way to intercept you on your way home. I had nothing better to do, so I came looking. Good thing I found you when I did. What happened?"

David stood, anchoring himself over his thighs, dragging in more fresh air.

"We should move back." Cade tugged David a good distance from his truck.

Now a blazing bonfire. What a complete waste.

Then his truck exploded. Dizziness swept over him. The world tilted. Cade assisted him to the ground. He gripped his aching head in his hands. He had a million other worries, but that…that was his truck. His new truck!

He felt Cade's squeeze on his shoulder. "I'm sorry, man. I know you loved it."

"It was only a truck." That was what he got for loving it. "Did you call for help?"

"First thing. I saw the flames and made the call."

Pulse racing, head pounding, David got to his feet again. That was too close.

"You scared me to death," Cade said.

Tracy hadn't been kidding when she'd said the people around her were in danger. Now David questioned the sanity of having her stay at Jewel's with so many other people who would be in danger. What had any of them been thinking? "Can you call Winters for me?"

"Sure, but do you think this is related to Tracy? To the grocery-store fire?"

"Absolutely."

Sirens erupted in the night. That sound happened too frequently of late for David's comfort, even though he was a fireman and should be accustomed to it. Lights flashed in the distance down the road as flames devoured David's truck, illuminating the surrounding area in a bright ring of light. Shadows danced in the forest around them. David peered into the woods. Was *he* still out there?

"Tell me," Cade said.

The words reminded David of their dad, who'd founded the Mountain Cove Avalanche Center. Ironically, he'd died in an avalanche.

"I was changing a flat tire and heard someone behind me. They struck me before I could react. I woke up in the burning truck."

The tanker truck arrived. Using the water in the two-thousand-pound tank, firefighters doused David's truck. Though it would have eventually burned out on its own, they wouldn't risk the fire spreading.

His firemen coworkers treated him with oxygen. Strange to be on this side of things, but he'd been here once before— the night his wife had died.

This event reminded him of all he'd lost. Little wonder he'd been dreaming about that night when he'd woken surrounded by flames. His body or mind had tried to warn him, bring him out of his unconscious state. That was the second time he'd been knocked out in a week. At this rate, he would end up with a traumatic brain injury like some jock professional football player.

Another vehicle turned onto the road. David recognized the cruiser. He would let Terry have it if he'd left Tracy unguarded. But then he saw Terry had a passenger. The police officer steered the cruiser over to the far side of the road, and Tracy jumped out of the vehicle before it had even come to a complete stop. She ran all the way to David and threw herself into his arms.

That stunned him. Filled him with pure joy he was too shocked to suppress. He savored it instead. After their conversation about keeping their distance, David was surprised at her action, but then he understood. That same force drove him to wrap his arms around her, pull her against him hard and breathe in the scent of her freshly washed hair. Try to soak in the goodness that was Tracy.

"Oh, David, I'm so sorry this happened." She sobbed into his shirt. "I couldn't stay away."

This was getting to be a habit with her. To be fair, she'd cried on him only twice now, but if she was going to cry into anyone's shoulders, it had better be his. His gut twisted. He'd become far more possessive than he had a right to be.

She pushed away, though not too far. "See, David? See what happens when you get involved with me? This is all my fault."

He held her face in his hands, weaving his fingers through the soft, wild hair behind her ears, and pulled her close so he could look her in the eyes.

"It's not your fault. It's this crazy man's fault. With every move he makes, he only makes it harder on himself. There isn't a person in town that won't be looking for him now, once they've heard what happened."

If only he could convince her that she shouldn't blame herself. Though he completely understood her thought process—he blamed himself for his wife's death.

Her eyes brimmed with concern, telling him things she felt about him that he knew she could never say, and stirred him to the bone. He wanted to kiss her again but instead he tugged her to him, wrapped his arms around her and held her soft, warm body tight against him. Funny, he was the victim this time, but here he was, reassuring her. No. He had that wrong. She *was* comforting him. The fact that she'd come to find him and run right into his arms made him crazy inside.

Crazy for her.

Another police vehicle pulled up. Winters.

David released Tracy, but held her hand, and she didn't resist. They were both crazy.

Chief Winters stepped out of his vehicle and made his way to David. He put his hands on his hips and surveyed the situation.

"What happened?" Winters asked.

David told him everything, except the dream, of course. But Winters had to know this sent David right back to the night Natalie had died.

"A close call. But not as close as it could have been." He eyed David.

David got his meaning, all right. He could have died. He was that close.

Winters took off his hat and adjusted the rim. "Looks like our assailant caught you off guard."

David understood what Winters wasn't saying. The man hadn't wanted David involved to begin with. Said it was police business, but David had insisted he needed to be part of protecting Tracy. Finally, Winters had relented, and look where that had gotten him?

How could David protect her when he couldn't even take care of himself?

Tracy had already caused Jewel enough trouble, so the next morning she decided to be up early and help Jewel serve breakfast. Maybe work would get her mind off the fact that David had almost died. She left Solomon in the room, promising to return after breakfast and take him on a long walk. Of course, she couldn't go alone, if at all. Still, he needed time to run off his energy after being cooped up in the room to avoid setting off Jewel's allergies. At least the woman had let Solomon stay as long as he kept to this room.

Jewel liked to serve a big breakfast around a table so folks could get to know one another before they headed their separate ways for their activities. Tracy had already made up a batch of wild-blueberry muffins and they baked in the oven, filling the kitchen and dining room with a wonderful aroma. She helped Jewel prepare her specialty dish, salmon quiche and reindeer sausage. Too robust a breakfast for Tracy, she snacked on fresh blueberries and began serving coffee and juice to the guests settled in at the large table.

A pass-through, a windowed counter in the wall separating the kitchen and dining room, allowed them to see and hear the guests. One place setting remained unattended, but breakfast was served at seven o'clock, regardless. Jewel pulled the muffins out and stuck more in, and together, Tracy and Jewel placed the serving dishes on the table.

Jewel winked at Tracy. "Let's say grace."

The ten guests present—believers or not—bowed their heads.

Though Jewel smiled when she finished, Tracy could tell she was on edge today. What had happened to David had them all jumpy. Tracy tried to talk to Jewel about moving out and away, but the woman shushed her and said they would talk later.

Maybe Tracy should leave without saying anything, but she couldn't do that to Jewel, either.

The final guest moseyed down the stairs and took the empty seat. Tracy hadn't seen him here before. Something about his appearance and demeanor made her feel uneasy. She needed to get a grip and calm her nerves. She was seeing bad guys everywhere she looked. Tracy made sure he got coffee, juice and the full meal deal, then moved on, her thoughts on everything except her task.

She needed a new cell. Using Jewel's phone, she'd made some calls to find Jennifer's number and finally left a voice mail for the marshal. Tracy hadn't heard back, which frustrated her beyond words. But what had she expected? The woman had a job to do and other witnesses to protect. Tracy had passed up her chance, and her indecision had to be driving the woman crazy, as well. Too much was happening. Tracy was too frazzled to think straight.

While the guests talked about their experiences so far and what was on their agendas for the day, Tracy served. Jewel mostly stayed in the kitchen, busy with food preparation. When Tracy poured more coffee into the new man's cup, she felt his dark eyes on her. She blinked up then back to her task when she realized she was missing the cup, pouring hot coffee on the table.

"Oh, I'm so sorry." She quickly wiped up the liquid from around his plate.

The man replied in an understanding tone, but she didn't register his words.

She went into the kitchen and came out with more muffins. Through her peripheral vision she could see him watching. Again.

"Are you finished? Can I get your plates?" she asked the twentysomething couple at the end of the table, clearly caught up in a world of their own.

They were in love. Anyone could see that. They simply nodded to Tracy. She scraped the plates away then dropped one of them on the tiled floor. It shattered.

Silence hung in the air.

Jewel quickly moved to her side and helped clean up the mess. Together, they carried the pieces of shattered glass along with the dishes Tracy hadn't broken to the kitchen and dumped them in the sink with a clank. Fortunately, the conversation in the dining room revived.

But now they had moved to discussing the killer. Someone brought up the car fire last night. It had happened where the B and B drive met the road, so she wasn't surprised they already knew. Or maybe they'd heard her talking with Jewel. Either way, news traveled fast.

Tracy stared at her shaking hands.

Taking Tracy's hand, Jewel pulled her to the far corner of the kitchen where no one else could see or hear. "What's the matter? Other than what we already know, of course."

"That man...the new guy," Tracy whispered. "What's his name?"

Jewel straightened. "Clarence Mercado. Why?"

"I don't know if it's anything, but... He was...watching me."

Jewel pursed her lips. "Do you think he's the one?"

Tracy covered her face. "I don't know. That sounds crazy."

Dropping her hands, she looked at Jewel's pale face. "Forget it. It can't be." Tracy had to sound crazy. She was being paranoid to think Jewel's new guest was after her.

"He's had this reservation for weeks now but, still, we should call the police." Jewel put her hand on the mounted wall phone. "Or better yet, I'll march out to the cruiser outside. Tell the officer we need him in here."

"No." Tracy pressed her hand over Jewel's. "I've caused you enough trouble. You'll never hear the end of this if this guy is just a guest and nothing more. Let's wait."

The thing was, most members in Santino's gang were covered with tattoos, including their faces—at least in the pictures Derrick had shown her. But not the guy sitting at the dining table. Yet Jay hadn't mentioned more than the one tattoo he'd seen on the wrist of the guy who had pushed him. She really was losing it.

"Wait?" Jewel lifted a brow. "For what?"

"Give me a few minutes." Tracy took a few calming breaths. "There's one way for me to know."

Jewel frowned, tilted her head. "How?"

"The tattoo. I need to see if it's there." Tracy kept her voice low.

Crossing her arms, Jewel leaned against the counter. "Could it be that the tattoo guy is onto the fact that you know to look for tattoos and he sent someone else to do his dirty work?"

Now, *that* made Tracy grin. "You've been reading too many mystery novels."

But the levity didn't last long, especially when Jewel eyed her. "This isn't a game."

"I know that." Better than Jewel did.

"Where is the tattoo and how do you intend to look for it? Tell me that, and I might give you two minutes before I call for help."

"I'm making it up as I go."

Without waiting for Jewel's reply, Tracy shoved through the swinging door connecting the two rooms. She didn't have a plan and she had to hurry.

God, please, let this guy just be ogling me because he's a creep, not because he's come to kill me or to hurt these people or to burn down this house.

When she put her prayer like that, she could see why Jewel wanted to call the police immediately. But it could be nothing.

Taking in a breath to steady her nerves, she approached the man. "More coffee?"

"Please," he said. He never took his eyes off her. If he wasn't a killer, he was downright rude. A jerk. And even if he was the guy sent to taunt her and kill her, why would he be so blatant about staring? Why didn't he just get on with the reason he was here?

Tracy decided she might enjoy this too much. She answered his stare with one of her own, feeling the flames from her past flashing in her eyes as she deliberately missed the coffee cup and poured hot coffee on his sleeve. "Do I know you, sir?"

He yelped and jerked out of the chair so fast, Tracy fell against the wall as she gasped.

Jewel broke through the kitchen door. "What's going on in here?"

Clarence Mercado released a string of what had to be profanity in Spanish, then glared at Tracy. She could swear he was about to take a step toward her, but everyone in the room had stopped to watch. This incident wouldn't look good in the online reviews of Jewel of the Mountain Bed and Breakfast.

The room was quiet as everyone watched and waited for something more to happen.

A fork clinked.

Clarence grabbed a napkin and wiped his arm off.

And Tracy held her breath.

The tattoo… She could see it on his wrist, just under the cuff of his sleeve. Her pulse rocketed.

Breathe. Just breathe.

She dared to look him in the eyes. In his dark gaze, she saw the thrill of his game. He *knew* she'd seen his tattoo.

FOURTEEN

David floored the gas pedal of the truck he'd borrowed from Cade. The truck rocked and bounced along the drive to the Jewel of the Mountain until the house came into view. He hadn't expected to see this many police vehicles lining the path.

David slammed the brakes.

The truck skidded, leaving marks in the grass, he was sure. But he didn't care. He jumped out and banged the door closed behind him. Running to the house, he hopped up the steps to the porch and barreled through the door.

"Tracy!"

Jewel appeared in the foyer. "She's upstairs."

He pressed by her.

She grabbed his arm. "Just calm down. She's fine. The police are here, as you can see. They're searching the woods."

David inhaled a long breath. Then another. Tracy didn't need to see him this upset. "You're sure she's okay?"

"Yes. She's on the phone...I think."

David's spirits sank. Jewel had been the one to call him, not Tracy herself. But what did he expect? "What happened?"

"He was here. The killer. Right here in my house. He

was here at breakfast. Kept looking at Tracy." Jewel's voice clogged with tears. "She's a bold one, that girl. She poured hot coffee on his arm to see if he had the tattoo."

David ground his molars. "That was a dangerous move. What about the other guests? Who was on duty to watch the house today? Why didn't you just call him or the police, Jewel?"

If David hadn't been at home nursing his concussion, he would have insisted on staying to guard the house himself.

"I wanted to get help, but what she said made sense. We had to know if the guy had the tattoo. He was wearing a long-sleeved shirt."

Wanting to go up to question Tracy himself, he glanced at the stairs, but thought better of it. "Then what happened?"

"He spouted off a few choice words in Spanish, and then a couple of the guys who'd left earlier in the morning came back for some gear. They were more burly than the other guests still at breakfast. I don't know if he would have done something different had they not showed up, but as soon as he saw them, he ran. He was out the door before we could stop him. Tracy..." Jewel shook her head. "I thought she'd collapse right there. We went into the kitchen and called the police. Then I went outside to find the officer in the cruiser and told him everything. He'd been instructed to watch for intruders. Not guests already staying."

Jewel pressed her face in her hands. Then, finally, she looked at David. "I'm so sorry this happened."

"It wasn't your fault. You couldn't have known or suspected your guest." But they were all to blame for this fiasco.

"I've never been so terrified, David. He could have

burned down my house." She grabbed David's arm. "But what am I saying? It's just a house. You could have died last night. Others would have died today. This old house can be rebuilt."

David understood what she'd meant. He'd lost his truck last night, but he could have lost his life. Or the killer could have chosen to target the B and B instead of David and his truck. Tracy, Jewel and all the other guests could have been killed.

"I appreciate you calling me to let me know."

Her concerned expression eased into a smile. "I knew you'd want to know. You should go up and see her."

Boots clomped on the front porch. Had they found the killer? David stiffened. Winters pushed through the screen door and into the foyer. He nodded to Jewel, his eyes lingering.

"Tell me," David said.

Winters frowned at David. Then his gaze traveled to the stairs, where Tracy took the last step down. "Chief Winters. What's going on? Did you get him?"

"Not yet. But we're closing in on him. He won't get away this time."

"Are you sure?" David asked. "Do you need more help in the search?"

"He's on foot. He can't go far. And he won't be leaving Mountain Cove by any other route. But just in case he decides to backtrack and come for you, I want you out of here." Winters's gaze flicked to Jewel and warmed. "You, too. Just for the rest of the day. I see this thing ending over the next few hours."

David didn't want to tell the man he was being far too hopeful, but maybe David would do better to cling to hope himself. He kept wondering about Tracy's phone call. Had she called the marshal? Was she going to leave Mountain Cove after all? Leave David?

Inside, his gut twisted. She wasn't his and he didn't deserve her or anyone. Didn't deserve a second chance. He couldn't protect himself, much less Tracy.

It was time to go. He shouldn't have come. He should let the police handle things.

"Well, then, it all sounds like things might get back to normal." David nodded at Jewel and turned to leave. He eyed Tracy, but she looked at the floor.

"Warren," Winters said. "Where do you think you're going?"

David hesitated at the door and turned. "What can I do for you?"

"Can you please escort these ladies to town? Keep them under your watchful eye? This isn't over yet. I don't have enough officers to search the region and guard Tracy, too."

"Of course." David should have offered, and he would have, but he was too busy protecting his own hide. His heart. Cad. But he wouldn't waste more time calling himself names. He turned to Jewel and Tracy. "Is there anything you want to grab before we leave?"

"Oh, no," Jewel said. "I can't leave yet. I need to keep the house open in case any of my guests return. Chief Winters, you can stay with me, can't you? And, Tracy, you gather what you need for the day and go with David."

Tracy hesitated. "I can't leave, either. I need to take Solomon out of the room for some fresh air."

"Oh, piffle. Let Solomon out of the room now. With this new development, he's free to wander the house." She winked at Tracy. "I'll take an allergy pill and then I can take him outside myself, or Chief Winters can help me. He's no problem."

Tracy didn't look convinced. "Are...you sure?"

"Of course. Solomon will be fine here with me. I can't leave, and there are too many police vehicles sitting outside. I doubt he'll come back."

"She's right." Winters maintained a serious demeanor but David didn't miss the twinkle in his eye.

"What about you, David?" Tracy asked. "You were set to leave. Am I keeping you from something?"

Funny they were both acting distant when just last night she'd run into his arms. And before that, they'd even shared a kiss. Then again, Tracy had her reasons for pushing him away, and he had his own, so he knew to keep his distance.

Still, he took a few steps closer and held out his hand. "Nothing that can't wait."

He bit back the urge to tell her the truth—that there was nothing he wanted to do more than be with her now. Slowly, as if measuring him, she placed her hand in his. He wanted to bring it to his lips and kiss it. But he resisted. She didn't need that from him, and he didn't deserve it.

David squeezed her hand and she felt the strength and warmth there. Took the reassurance that he offered.

"This will be over soon," he said. "You're going to be okay."

The words reminded her of their reassurances to Jay when he was hanging on to his life on the ridge. Was this David's training talking, trying to keep her calm, or did he really believe what he'd said? She studied him, searching the depths behind his forest green eyes, wanting his words to mean more to him. But even if they did, Tracy had been the one to close that door.

Dark shadows outlined his eyes. That had to be from his close call last night. But his haggard look didn't detract from his strong, handsome features. Myriad emotions swelled in her chest, and Tracy wanted to run to him, to pull him to her, much as she'd done last night when he'd nearly died. She wanted to rest her head against his chest and hear the steady beat of his strong heart inside. Her own heart grateful for his survival.

God, thank You for saving him.

The outcome could have been much different. How could he stand there and offer his help when she'd brought so much trouble to this town? And to David personally?

"Let me just grab my pack." She bounded up the stairs to her room and hugged Solomon, offering reassurance that she would return. When she opened the door to let him out, he just sat there and stared at her.

Tracy threw a few items into her backpack. No telling how this day would play out. She might need an extra set of clothes. She wasn't as certain as Winters they would catch the killer today, but she wholeheartedly agreed she shouldn't stay here.

Solomon's sad brown eyes tugged at her heartstrings. She rubbed him behind the ears. "Look, I don't know what today will bring, so I can't take you. But I promise to come back, okay?"

At least she'd put in another call to Jennifer a few minutes ago, after the incident at breakfast, and explained everything that had happened last night and today.

On voice mail.

If she was in serious trouble, well, then, Tracy certainly couldn't count on any immediate help from the marshals. But she reminded herself that she'd been the one to venture out on her own. And she had the support of this whole amazing town behind her.

Tracy led Solomon out of the room and down the stairs, where she told him to be good. In the foyer, Tracy caught

David leaning against the wall. Though he was waiting for Tracy, he was watching Jewel and Chief Winters deep in conversation. Tracy smiled to herself. Was there something going on between those two? Jewel deserved a good man, if she wanted one.

David turned his attention to Tracy, his eyes lighting up. "You ready?"

"As I'll ever be."

Once they sat inside the truck, David started it up but he didn't go anywhere. He turned to face Tracy. "Are you okay?"

She blew out a breath. "I'm still frazzled. To think I was that close to the killer. The man who hurt Jay and killed Veronica, who set your truck on fire last night and tried to kill you."

"But to pour coffee on him like that, Tracy…"

"Ah, so Jewel told you about that." Her cheeks warmed. That had been a bold move on her part.

"I don't think you should have done it. You could have gotten yourself killed. Jewel, too, and her guests."

"I slept in the same house with him last night, David. He made it through our guard. We didn't even think to pay such close attention to the new guest. And then he stared at me through breakfast, like it was all some sick game to him. He was here to toy with me. Hurt people as a way to torture me. I didn't think I was pushing it to find out the truth." She put the window down and sucked in fresh air. "Can we just go now?"

"I don't know if you feel up to this, but I thought we'd go see Jay today."

"In Juneau?"

"Sure. Why not? We'll be far away from here."

"You mean where I should have been days ago. Far away."

"No, that's not what I mean. We want you to stay, Tracy. The town, we stand behind you."

"Can you really speak for the town?" *And what about you? Do you stand behind me?* But she knew the answer.

"Yes, I think I can. People have gone out of their way to tell me."

"And why not me?"

"You're isolated up here. People have more access to me."

She had to admit, she felt more welcome here than she'd ever felt in her hometown in Missouri. She wasn't sure the town where she grew up would be this supportive. But that was all the more reason to feel guilt over putting all these people in danger.

Should she leave again? "I called her, David."

"Marshal Hanes?"

"Yes."

David blew out a breath. "What are you going to do?"

"I got voice mail. Told her there was a manhunt for the killer. He could be caught today."

"But?"

She smiled to herself. He somehow always knew there was more to her story. "This guy is just one of thousands of gang members Santino can order around from prison. If my location isn't secret anymore, then more of them could come. I'll see how today goes and then decide."

"Tracy, what's really keeping you here? I…want the best for you. I don't even know what that is."

Tracy was surprised David had asked. She wasn't sure what to say. Any answer she would give him would be the wrong one. She couldn't give him false hope by telling him he was one of the reasons she wanted to stay, and yet, leaving him out of the equation would also hurt him. She could sense that much. They'd agreed a relationship couldn't go anywhere, and here she was, sitting in his vehicle again. Oh, wait. This wasn't his vehicle, considering what had happened to David's truck last night. If she remembered correctly, this truck looked like his brother Cade's.

The images from last night flared in her thoughts once again and her heart squeezed. Her fault. He'd almost lost his life and he *had* lost his truck. He loved that truck, too. She could tell. So many small things she already knew about him. And liked.

"A lot…just a lot is keeping me here, okay? You already know I'm tired of running. Let's go see Jay. We can talk more on the way."

David steered out the drive, slowly maneuvering around the potholes. Jewel had a beautiful and well-tended bed-and-breakfast but the drive begged for attention. Once they met the real road, David turned to head back to town. He got on his cell and phoned Billy to see if he could meet them at the floatplane dock for a quick trip to Juneau.

Tracy looked out the window and smiled to herself. Must be nice to have such easy access to travel in Southeast Alaska, almost as though David had his own bush pilot on call.

When they drove by the spot where David's truck had burned, the wreckage had been towed off. He kept his gaze straight ahead and didn't look. Probably didn't welcome the reminder, and wanted to think about something else. Tracy noticed he frowned now and then, as though in pain, and she remembered he must be suffering from a headache from being knocked unconscious.

Something in the woods caught her attention. She sat up, wondering if David had seen it, too.

She glanced his way. He was still on the phone, but he appeared to have lost interest in the conversation.

Someone ran out into the center of the road to stand directly in their path.

It was the man who'd called himself Clarence Mercado.

He aimed a weapon at them.

FIFTEEN

A man stood in the road, aiming his weapon at the windshield.

At Tracy.

Police spilled from the forest shouting, pointing guns at the man. It all happened before David could blink.

"Get down!" David called out. He reached over and pressed Tracy's head down toward her knees, shielding her as he swerved. He wanted to veer to the right, putting his side of the vehicle in harm's way, but Mountain Cove police were in the path, forcing him to swerve left.

Not good.

Gunfire erupted. A bullet shattered the window on the passenger's side. Another bullet ripped through the door.

Tracy screamed.

A tree loomed in David's vision. He swerved and slowed, but Cade's top-heavy vehicle rolled to the side and then over. The airbags exploded.

Seconds ticked by before David shook off his daze, his mind racing to catch up with what had happened.

"Tracy!" He pushed the layers of nylon away, unbuckled his seat belt and reached for her.

Hanging upside down, secured in her position by her seat belt, she didn't move.

"Tracy, wake up." *Lord, please let her be okay.*

He pushed more of the deflated airbag out of the way and angled her face toward him. He felt her pulse. Strong.

Chief Winters pulled open the passenger's-side door. "An ambulance is on the way."

"Tracy," David said. "Come on—wake up."

When he pulled his hand back, it was covered in blood.

Panic sent his heart tripping. He didn't want to move her, but it was difficult to examine her where she was pinned to the seat, held there by the taut seat belt.

God, show me where she's injured. His heart and mind scrambled for traction—she'd been hurt on his watch. Then he found the gunshot wound on her arm, and without moving her too much, he examined it more closely. Looked as though she'd been grazed was all. He pulled off his shirt to stanch the flow of blood.

Had she hit her head when the vehicle rolled or was there another injury? His hands shook, even as he kept his shirt pressed in place and prayed softly. Finally, Tracy's eyelashes fluttered.

She sighed and then groaned. Opening her eyes, she blinked, frowning. Her position was awkward to say the least.

"What…? Where am I?" Her blue irises focused on David. "What happened?"

"The killer tried…" He couldn't say the word. "Almost succeeded."

She closed her eyes. "What happened to him?"

"He's dead." Winters spoke from outside the truck. "Couldn't be helped."

Tracy breathed a sigh of relief. "Any chance I can get out of the truck? The blood is rushing to my head."

"We're waiting on the ambulance and the EMTs before we move you," David said.

She squinted at him. "Aren't you a paramedic?"

How did he tell her his heart rate soared, making his chest hurt? How could he tell her didn't trust himself? Why did he keep trying?

And failing.

Unexpectedly she reached up and put her hand against his cheek.

"David? Are you all right?" She searched his gaze with more intensity than David could stand.

He sucked in a breath. "I thought I'd lost you."

"But you didn't. I'm right here. Are you going to help me out, or what?"

He grinned. "Maybe I can manage that after all."

Sirens blared in the distance. Were others injured, as well? David had failed to ask about them; his focus was on Tracy. "I'm going to release the seat belt. Brace yourself."

But he had every intention of catching her when he released her.

The seat belt didn't want to budge. David whipped out his pocketknife and cut her out. Then she fell against him.

His heart warmed. Releasing a grateful, heartfelt sigh of relief, he was glad she couldn't see his face, and he didn't resist pressing into her neck, breathing her in. If she noticed, she didn't say anything, didn't resist.

"It wasn't your fault." She held on to him as though she could feel his pain, but she didn't know about the trauma from his past.

"You're hurt. I should have done something differently."

"Shh," she said. "It's over now. If Clarence—or whoever he was—is dead now, then it's over."

She'd stiffened, ever so slightly, when she'd said the

words. He should have been the one comforting her. Some hero, some protector, he was.

But was it really over? He wanted to believe that, but he couldn't quite trust in it yet. Even if it wasn't, at least they had a reprieve.

He assisted Tracy out of Cade's damaged truck.

The EMTs took her to check her over, but David stayed nearby. Winters huddled with the police officers as the killer was put into a body bag. Who was this guy, really? Was he working for Santino, as Tracy had said? Why hadn't he tried to kill her last night if he stayed in the B and B? Or had the incident at breakfast forced his hand today, making him move up his timeline? They might never get those answers, now that he was dead.

David shook his head at the sight of Cade's truck.

"That makes two this week." Cade stood next to him, surprising him with his appearance. News traveled fast.

David blew out a breath. "I'm sorry, bro."

Cade trudged closer and looked at the damage. "I'm just glad you're okay, for the second time in twenty-four hours. But you've had—what?—two concussions in a few days. I'm concerned about you."

"Don't be. I'm hardheaded." The symptoms had faded. The concussions were mild, thankfully. Besides, he couldn't rest until this was over.

More vehicles pulled up, crunching gravel. Footfalls resounded. Adam, Isaiah, Heidi and Cade's wife, Leah, joined them.

"Where's little Scott?" David asked. A crime scene wasn't the place for a child, but it wasn't as if they could leave a two-month-old baby alone.

"Grandma gave us a break for a couple of hours," Leah said. "We were heading off to lunch when we heard."

"And I just destroyed your time alone." David sent Cade an apologetic look.

Leah blew out a breath and grabbed her husband's hand. "It's okay, David. We're just glad this wasn't much worse."

"Who's in the body bag?" Heidi asked, her tone grim.

"The killer, and he almost killed Tracy this time." David glanced back to make sure she was being examined. He caught her gaze as they shoved the gurney all the way in. "I have to go."

He left his family behind and caught up with the EMT. "Whoa, there. What's happening? Is she going to be all right?"

"Sure. Just taking her to the hospital to treat that gunshot wound. Get an X-ray or two. You might think of doing the same thing. You look a little banged up yourself."

He was fine. "Can I ride with you?"

The EMT quirked a grin. "If you don't think you're needed here, then no problem."

After a quick glance in Chief Winters's direction, David confirmed the man was busy. He'd been there and had seen things unfold for himself, as had his officers, and didn't necessarily need a statement from David or Tracy. He could always track them down if he did. David gave the EMT a nod to thank him for letting him ride to the hospital with Tracy. It paid to have friends in town. He climbed up and into the back of the ambulance. Tracy's eyes widened.

"Mind if I come along?" He found a place to sit before she could reply.

"Of course not." She tried to smile, but he could see she was in pain from her gunshot wound, and likely the shock to her body was catching up to her.

He ignored his own aches and pains. They weren't anything serious.

Thank You, Lord, that it wasn't much worse.

He tried to still the churning in his gut, and he grinned, hoping to hide his grim mood. He wished he could believe Tracy when she'd said that this was all over, but he knew she'd said that for his benefit. She'd already told him it would never end.

Before the EMT climbed inside, David leaned close, ran his thumb down her cheek. "I'm sorry this happened."

She smiled, softly. "I'm glad it wasn't worse and that you weren't badly injured. I couldn't live with myself if even one more person got hurt because of me."

If she only knew how he related to that sentiment.

"I know what I said earlier." She averted her eyes. "But we can't be sure this is over."

Then her gaze found him again.

He took her hand. "I know."

He wanted to tell her he would see this through with her, but doubt coursed through him. Was he the best man for the job?

"If one more thing happens, then I'm leaving."

His breath hitched. "You mean…"

She nodded. "WITSEC. I can't watch anyone else get hurt. I have to leave Mountain Cove forever. My family. And I have to leave…"

When she didn't voice the rest, he thought he read it in her eyes.

You.

While she programmed her new cell phone, Tracy stared out the window of her room at the bed-and-breakfast main house, looking at what little she could see of the cottage through the trees. She'd already texted her mother with the new number. She had no idea how Santino had found her in Mountain Cove to begin with, so getting a new phone and number was for the best. Still, she hadn't gotten a new address.

As for her mother, Tracy would call her later, but she didn't want to get into a long conversation just now when she was expecting David any minute.

Solomon rested his chin on the windowsill and whined. She ran her hand over his head and behind the thick fur of his ear. "I know, boy, I know."

He'd had much more freedom to roam when they'd lived in the cottage. Should she move back in, give Jewel a chance to rent this room out? Except Tracy didn't know if it was a good idea. She didn't know if she was safe or not. Or ever would be.

Chief Winters was still conducting the investigation. He seemed to believe that Mercado had come to town to taunt Tracy by harming others, repeating what she and Derrick had gone through before. Then, when his cover was blown and he'd run out of options with the police closing in on him, he'd attempted to finish the job. That was their theory, anyway.

Tracy wished they could have faked her death, somehow, so that no one else would be dispensed to come and get her now that Santino knew where she was. Chief Winters was working with other law-enforcement entities to keep Santino's men from returning, but she wasn't sure how he could be so confident that it wouldn't happen again.

It made her head ache even more to think about a life spent living in fear, looking over her shoulder. And her arm still ached where she'd been shot. The doctor said it would take a few weeks to heal completely. She'd been fortunate the bullet had only grazed her.

Solomon barked at the door. Tracy smiled and opened it just as David was about to knock. "Jewel sent me on up," he said. "I hope you don't mind."

"Not at all."

"Are you ready?"

"Sure." They'd never made it to see Jay and he was scheduled to be released from the hospital next week, surprising them all. But he'd had no back, head or internal injuries. Still, the road to recovering with so many broken bones would take weeks. Tracy was certain he would be glad to recover at home with his family.

Family… Tracy sighed, missing her own family.

Solomon whined again. "You can't come. I'm sorry." To David, she said, "I took Solomon for a walk. He hates being cooped up in the room."

"So let him out. Jewel doesn't care."

"I know, but he knocked a vase over. One of the guests threw a ball and he caught it. They should have been outside. So, I don't want him bothering anyone."

"Let's take him and drop him off at my grandmother's house. She'd welcome the company, and he'd have a little room to roam."

"Oh, no. I couldn't trouble her."

"No trouble at all, Tracy. And in fact, I've been thinking about something."

"Yeah?"

"Wasn't sure when to bring it up, but now is as good a time as any."

Tracy eased into the chair at the desk, both smiling and a little wary.

"I don't think you should stay here anymore. At least, until we're sure this is over."

"I've been thinking the same thing." But she wasn't sure she was ready to stay in the cottage. Not yet.

"No, I don't think you have been."

She cocked her head, unsure what he meant or if she wanted to know. "I've already told you if anything else happened that I'm going into WITSEC."

Frowning, he nodded and moved to stare out the window. His reaction wasn't any surprise. He'd told her on more than one occasion he didn't want her to leave, but he had to be feeling the burden of having her around, too, the same as Chief Winters and the rest of the town.

"When my mother died, over two decades ago, Grandma Katy moved in to care for us and she never left. We all think of it as her house, and we all used to live there. Cade got married and moved out, and the same with Heidi when she married Isaiah a few months ago."

A deep, painful sigh eased from David. Tracy wanted to know what brought on the palpable pain emanating from him. He hadn't mentioned when he'd moved out, but it had probably been after his own marriage. Was he thinking about his wife? Tracy had learned that she'd died, but she didn't know the details.

She understood that kind of pain. She'd felt it after losing Derrick. They hadn't made it to the altar yet, but she had pictured herself with Derrick forever. She'd thought that they were getting close, that he might propose... And then he'd gotten involved in his research to write a dangerous investigative article and Santino had taken him from her.

"David?" She knew his thoughts were far away, and snagged his attention back. "What are you suggesting?"

"That you could stay with her in the house. She's all alone. Or even live in the apartment above the garage— that's where Cade used to live. You wouldn't have to go back to the cottage, it's too isolated, and Jewel wouldn't have to worry about her guests being in danger."

"But what about your grandmother?"

"She'd be fine—all her neighbors look out for her. You'd be closer to town and in a neighborhood. We all live close. It's safer than out here…and it's just in case."

David already knew she planned to leave if she had even a hint that someone else would come for her. Mountain Cove had already paid too high a price as it was, and yet it was for that very reason that she couldn't simply run after someone had lost their life on her account. But how could she stay if it cost them even more?

Her cell rang. She eyed the caller ID. Her mother. Tracy sighed. "How much time do we have before we have to leave?" she asked David.

He glanced at his watch. "Five minutes if we want to make it in time. Billy doesn't like to wait."

Tracy answered. "Mom, hi. I—"

"Tracy, it's your father."

Her mother's voice was shaky, tearful.

Tracy's knees shook. "What's happened?"

Her mother started bawling, trying to speak through the tears. Tracy couldn't understand the words. She felt David's arms around her, supporting her.

"Tracy, this is Carol." Tracy's sister sighed. "We've been trying to reach you. It's Dad. He was beaten and is in the hospital."

"Beaten? What do you mean? How bad is it?"

"I don't want to talk on the phone, but you're so far away. It was…bad. Can you come?"

"Is he going to…?"

"Live. He's going to live, but he's asking for you."

Oh, how she'd missed her family. If she'd gone into WITSEC, she wouldn't have the opportunity to see them ever again, even if someone took ill or was near death. But then again…maybe if she'd left for good this wouldn't have happened. Was the attack against her father from Santino, too?

"Why? Why would someone do that?"

God, please let it be for some reason other than the obvious.

"The police don't know. It appears to be a random beating."

"I'm coming. Text me the details."

She ended the call, hurt and anger boiling inside.

"What is it? Tracy, tell me what's going on." David's voice barely registered, but she was grateful for his presence.

"It's my dad. Someone beat him—he's in the hospital. I have to go." The police might have thought it was random, but Tracy knew this nightmare would never end for her unless she could somehow wake up. "Santino has targeted my family now, too."

And waking from this nightmare meant someone had to die.

Tracy or Santino had to die.

SIXTEEN

David righted his seatback as the 747 prepared for landing in St. Louis, Missouri. Tracy's seat next to him was empty—she'd gone to the restroom. He stared out the window, watching as they approached the city. The flight seemed to have taken much too long to get there.

He'd been surprised that Tracy hadn't balked when he'd insisted on coming with her. But she'd had no one else and was too shaken up to travel alone. David imagined she'd agreed because she'd been so distraught upon hearing about her father and hadn't had much fight left for anything else. Besides, she'd known he wouldn't take no for an answer.

All it had taken was grabbing a few essentials. Billy had already been waiting to fly them to Juneau, where they'd bought tickets to travel the rest of the way.

He scratched his rough chin, thinking he might have forgotten his razor. He really didn't know what he was doing in all this. The moment he'd learned she was in danger, he'd assigned himself as her personal protector. A woman he'd wanted to avoid. A woman who seemed determined to push him away.

David wondered who would be his protector when it came to his heart, because he wasn't doing a good job.

Seeing her anguish at the news of her father had twisted his gut into a knot. He was into her in a way he'd never intended. But it wasn't as if he could bail on her now. He'd see this through and keep her safe.

The plane shifted, angling to the right. Where was Tracy, anyway?

He frowned, wishing she would come back to her seat. He rubbed his forehead, feeling the exhaustion of the past few days pressing down on him.

She was still in danger. What he didn't know was how to keep her safe, how to stop the man running things from prison. Why didn't the authorities have more power to stop this? One of the problems was getting them to believe it was all connected in the first place. Law enforcement, along with any government entity, seemed to move with the speed of a raft across the Pacific.

She'd told him that if something else happened— someone else was hurt—she would leave Mountain Cove for good and go into WITSEC. He didn't know if this event counted because it hadn't even happened in Mountain Cove.

God, please let it not count.

But what was he thinking? He was being selfish.

Tracy returned to her seat and buckled in. When her gaze bounced off David and then went to the window, he saw the torment in her eyes. Reaching for her hand, he held it and squeezed. There weren't any words for this situation, and holding her hand was all he could think to do. She squeezed back and seemed to take strength from him.

With his other hand, he gripped the hand rest as the plane came in for the landing.

"David," she said.

"Yeah?"

"Thank you."

He turned his face to her. In her eyes, he saw her gratitude, and it nearly undid him. When this was all over, he didn't have a clue how he would extricate his heart, but he knew it would be painful. Maybe even for her, too.

"You're welcome."

After they landed and disembarked, Tracy's sister, Carol, met them outside the terminal. Carol was a tall, slender woman with black hair who didn't look as if she could be related to Tracy.

Tracy introduced David. "He's…a friend and, well…"

"I didn't want her to travel alone. I just came along to help," he added. But he could tell by the look in Carol's eyes she thought something was going on between them. Regardless, she didn't say anything as she drove them directly to the hospital.

David and Tracy followed Carol down the sterile hallways and up the elevator. Once they approached the door to Tracy's father's room, David hesitated. This was a family affair.

He decided he wouldn't join her in the room and she didn't even look back as she entered. Her focus was on her father, as it should be. He prayed the man would recover quickly. Though he should wait to hear more news about what had happened, he chose to head to the waiting room area and make the calls he hadn't had a chance to make.

He called Cade first. He told him everything, suggesting he keep an eye out and check on Jewel and on Tracy's dog.

Then he called Winters. "Warren, I don't have time for you to call me every day. We're wrapping up this investigation, anyway."

"I'm in Missouri with Tracy. This isn't over yet."

"What happened?"

"Her father was brutally beaten within an inch of his life."

"I'll contact the investigating officer and find out what they know, but obviously that's out of my jurisdiction."

"Tracy thinks it's related. That her family has been targeted."

"Tracy should go into WITSEC, if it's not too late."

David blew out a breath. Not what he wanted to hear.

"Anyone with eyes can see you have a thing for her, but if you want what's best for her, you'll talk her into it. It's the only way for her to be safe."

"But you assured her that the Mountain Cove police would protect her."

"And she's not in Mountain Cove anymore, is she? For that matter, neither are you."

David was surprised to note that his hand shook. He couldn't believe what Winters was telling him. Maybe David had known this was the only way all along, but his mind hadn't wanted to go there. He glanced across the waiting room and saw Tracy searching for him. Before he could react, her gaze found him and she closed the distance.

For a third time, Tracy pressed her face into his shoulder and sobbed.

Tracy sat in the chair next to her father's bed.

When she'd first seen him earlier in the week, he'd reminded her of how Jay had looked in the hospital. So many bandages she could hardly recognize him. One side of her father's face remained bandage-free and was black-and-blue.

"Oh, Dad," she whispered, tears in her throat.

It had been all she could do to hold it together at the sight of him, though Carol had warned her about the severity of the injuries. Fortunately, her own gunshot wound

was safely bandaged and easily hidden beneath her clothing, so no one asked her any questions.

But nobody could have prepared her to see her father
this way. Someone in the family remained by his side at all
times in case he needed anything, despite the nursing staff.
She'd given her mother and sister a break to go home and
shower and eat, and then they'd be back. David was staying
with Carol and Tim, in their extra room, and Carol would
bring him to the hospital later this morning.

Tracy still couldn't believe he'd come with her. He'd
promised to stick with her until this was over and, apparently, he was a man of his word. She wasn't sure how
she felt about that. One thing she did know: she felt safe
and protected with him near her.

"Tracy." Her father's voice was weak. He held out his
hand.

Tracy reached for it. There was none of the usual
strength in his grip. "Dad, I'm so sorry."

"Not your fault."

She wasn't so sure. She didn't want to argue with him,
and maybe he already knew. "Who did this, Dad?"

"Already told the police. Don't know."

"Did you see a tattoo?"

"Happened too fast."

She squeezed his hand again. She wouldn't ask him more
questions. She already knew—this was part of Santino's
retaliation. When she was in protection while waiting for
the trial, she'd agreed to be a witness, regardless, but she'd
extracted a promise that she could go into WITSEC at any
time after the trial should it become clear that Santino would
try to harm her or her family. Her father, however, had never
agreed. Would he now?

"Dad, there's something we need to talk about."

"I can guess what that is." He coughed.

Oh, God, help me to convince him.

"Santino sent someone to Mountain Cove to try to kill me."

Her father squeezed her hand. "Why didn't you tell me?"

"I know I should have. Then maybe you could have avoided this. Been more alert. But the man was killed. And now this. Dad…"

"I won't live in fear. I won't lose everything I've worked for."

"What about your life?" David's voice surprised her.

He came all the way in the room. In his gaze, she saw his apology for interrupting.

"Dad, this is my friend from Mountain Cove. David Warren."

Her father's one-eyed bloodshot gaze looked at David. Sized him up. "What are you to my daughter?"

"Dad!" Tracy stood, feeling the heat creep up her neck. "He's my friend, that's all. He's a fireman and search-and-rescue volunteer in Mountain Cove. A real hero." He'd come along to protect her and didn't deserve to be grilled by her father. But she'd said more than she should, making it sound as if they were more than friends, her words defensive, protesting too much.

The way David looked at her, with appreciation and something much more, as though he could reach across the room and wrap her in his arms with his gaze alone, sent warmth and longing through her. What they had between them was much more than friendship, but she had to shut those feelings down. The ways things looked, she would always live in fear of her life. And caring about him was a big mistake. She couldn't go through losing someone again.

"Back to what David said, Dad. Your business isn't

worth your life." Or her mother's. Or her own. Didn't he understand that she wouldn't change her identity and life without him? He was risking all their lives.

The nurse came in to check his vitals and Tracy took the opportunity to leave the room with David. Out in the hall she said, "Where's Carol? Didn't she bring you?"

"No. I rented a car. Didn't want to be in the way, and I wanted to be free to come up here when I needed to."

Tracy shook her head. "I'm sorry about all this. You don't have to stay, you know. You have a job to do in Mountain Cove."

"This is more important. I want you to be safe." He enclosed her hand in his. "What are you going to do?"

"I don't know."

His gaze emanated more concern for her than she deserved. More than she could handle. That first day when she'd seen her father, she'd kept it together until she'd left his room. All she could think about was finding David and losing herself in his protective arms. And then she'd sobbed into his shirt. Again. She wanted to be in his arms right now, too. But she had to maintain her composure, and she was getting too attached to this guy. Something she couldn't allow.

"All I know is that I want this nightmare to be over."

David took her in his arms then and weaved his fingers into her hair. With his arms wrapped around her, she felt as though she was cocooned in protection. That he cared deeply for her was evident. Even though she'd warned him they should keep their distance, he was here, helping her through this. And she hadn't resisted.

Somehow she had to regain clarity. Think things through. Figure out what to do about her family to keep them safe. Figure out how to protect her heart.

She pulled away. "I need to splash water on my face,

freshen up. Would you mind hanging out here until I get back or Carol or Mom gets here?"

"Of course not." Studying her, he frowned. "You think someone might try to harm him while he's in the hospital?"

She stared at the floor. "I hope not. But try convincing the police to put someone at his door when they think it was a random act of violence."

The investigative wheels moved much too slowly to make a difference for Tracy and her family, and anyone else who dared to get too close, such as David.

Tracy watched him go back into her father's room and she went to the restroom, washed her hands and brushed her hair. She looked a mess and that embarrassed her, though she shouldn't care what David thought of her. Closing her eyes, she took a few calming breaths and headed back to the hospital room. Tracy peeked in on her father and David, deep in a discussion about the oil business, and decided to head to the first floor to grab coffee for her and David. In the elevator she was alone until the second floor, when a woman stepped on, dressed in long-sleeved scrubs. Behind the woman's ear was a tattoo. Numbers. What did they mean?

Heart pounding, Tracy tried to slow her breathing. The tattoo could mean nothing. Or everything. She wished Derrick had never gone so deep in his research. Wished he'd backed away from his article. Tracy wished she knew nothing at all about gang tattoos. That way she wouldn't be wondering if those numbers behind the woman's ear had anything to do with the number of people she'd harmed.

Glancing down, Tracy stared at the floor, allowing her gaze to flick to the woman's wrist. She caught a glimpse of *the* tattoo.

Tracy couldn't breathe.

SEVENTEEN

Carol and Gina, Tracy's mom, entered the room. Tracy's father was sleeping. David had grown impatient for Tracy to return, but she'd appeared to need a break and he'd given her that. Surely she was safe in a hospital. But she hadn't answered her phone. He knew she'd be upset if he left her father for even one second, so he was glad to see her mother and sister.

"Where's Tracy?" Gina asked.

"She went to freshen up." David stood. "I'll find her."

He didn't see her in the waiting room or down the hallway, so he knocked on the door of the women's restroom. Finally another woman approached the entrance and frowned at him.

"Could you check for me? Ask if Tracy is inside."

Her frown softened. "Sure, I'll look."

A few seconds later she returned. "Sir, there's no one in the restroom."

He hadn't thought she'd stay in there so long. David hurried to the elevator. Maybe she'd gone down to grab snacks or coffee. But he would think she would answer the phone. The hospital elevators took entirely too long.

He made the first-floor main lobby and hurried to the small shop where they'd spotted the snacks and coffee.

No Tracy. Unsure if this was an actual emergency, he opted for calling the police detective who'd left his card on the side table next to Tracy's father's bed in case the man thought of something more. David had snagged the card on his way out of the room in case he needed it. He wasn't all that sure that the police were the right entities to handle this. Organized crime, including gangs, warranted the attention of the Department of Justice or the FBI at the very least. But the police were always the first to handle things until they escalated.

So what about now? What about the attempts on her life? Winters was right. She needed to run and hide.

Phone to his ear, he stood in the lobby, watching for her and praying.

The elevator door swooshed open.

A woman stepped out—hospital staff, by her dress—but no Tracy.

David got the detective's voice mail and ended the call. He wasn't sure what he would say. Not yet. He tried her cell again and got no response. All he could think was that her phone had better be dead. She might be back in her father's room by now. Unwilling to wait on the slow-moving elevators, David took the stairwell this time and on the second floor stood Tracy, pale-faced and huddled in the corner.

David grabbed her shoulders. "Tracy, what's wrong?"

"They're here."

"Who? Who's here?" But he already knew the answer.

"Members of Santino's gang. There was someone dressed in scrubs, either working at the hospital or pretending to work. She had the tattoo." Tracy appeared dazed and shocked, which concerned David more than anything at the moment. "She got on the elevator with me. I don't know if she wanted to harm me because a security officer got on the elevator at the next floor. I got off just as he got on."

"And why are you in the stairwell?"

Her gaze locked with his and a small smile seemed to shake off the dazed look. "I could ask you the same thing."

"The elevators are too slow."

"You don't have to tell me. Those were the longest three minutes of my life. When I got off the elevator I just wanted to hide, so I slipped into the stairwell."

"I was worried about you when you didn't come back or answer your phone. I had to find you." He hugged her to him. She could have been killed on that elevator, right here in the hospital. "We need to call the detective, tell him everything. Your dad needs protection."

"I tried to call but the cell won't work in the stairwell," she said.

That explained why he hadn't been able to get through to her. He tightened his hold on her, fearing he could lose her forever. He couldn't go through that again. He planted a kiss on the top of her head, hoping she didn't mind, but it wasn't exactly a *real* kiss, as they'd shared before. The kind that he'd promised never to give her again.

Even through this dangerous scenario, David hadn't stopped thinking about the kiss they'd shared. He was torturing himself on that one. He couldn't let himself love her.

"David," she whispered.

"Yes."

"You can let me go now. We need to check on Dad. Call the police."

Slowly he released her and looked down into her eyes.

"Don't go anywhere else alone—that is, until you're safe and sound in WITSEC and have a whole new life."

At the words, a knot lodged in his throat.

She shook her head. "Didn't you hear my father? He's not going, which means I'm not going."

"But this is insane. It will never stop. You said if anything else happened you would leave Mountain Cove and start a new life as a new person."

"I meant if anything happened in Mountain Cove." She grabbed her hair. "I'm so confused, I don't know what to do. But I'm going back to Mountain Cove. Maybe this happened to my father because Mercado was killed instead of me, and this was a warning. If possible, we need to draw them away from my family."

Protect her family by putting *herself* right back in the line of danger? Yeah. As if that made a whole lot of sense. Couldn't someone do something to stop this kind of criminal activity? When David exited the stairwell with Tracy, his cell phone rang. Detective Palmer. David answered the call and explained everything as he and Tracy made their way to her father's room. At the door to the room, David ended his conversation with the detective.

"What did he say?" she asked.

"He's coming to the hospital to question you. It sounds like he's taking this more seriously now. Should you let Marshal Hanes know about these new developments?"

"Why? It won't change a thing. My father refuses to leave his life and, by default, I refuse to leave my life in Mountain Cove."

Her words terrified David. Winters was right. He had to convince her to go into WITSEC. "Are you sure that's a good idea?"

"I'm not helping my family by staying here. And this time I want to face the threat head-on."

* * *

They stood at the door of David's grandmother's home and knocked.

As soon as she'd made sure her father was on the road to recovery, she'd returned to Mountain Cove—in part, she hoped to draw attention back to her and away from her family. In addition, the detective had discovered solid leads regarding who had assaulted her father and assured her arrests would be made. In the meantime, he'd stationed police to guard her father's room.

Her mother had hired a firm to beef up security around the house. Tracy should be relieved, but she couldn't help but wonder how long they would have to live like this.

David smiled. "I could just walk in. She's family, after all. I used to live here."

He reached for the knob just as the door opened. An older woman's face brightened with a huge smile. "Oh, David. So wonderful to see you."

The woman hugged David to her as she pulled them both inside the house. Then she turned her attention on Tracy. "And this is the woman you were telling me about?"

David looked at Tracy with admiration in his eyes. "This is my friend Tracy Murray. And this is Grandma Katy," David said to Tracy.

Tracy thrust her hand forward. "I'm pleased to meet you."

"Oh, dear, we hug around here." The woman tugged her into an embrace. "And you can call me Katy."

The warm and friendly woman released Tracy. A lump grew in Tracy's throat. "Katy, then."

Katy continued her conversation with David as she led them into an open living room connected to the kitchen. Inside the cozy home, Tracy noticed the same cross-stitched scriptures on the walls that Jewel had in the cottage and in her house. Tracy couldn't help but feel slightly awkward. After all, not even a month ago she'd avoided David Warren, thought he was cold and aloof, and now here she was, already meeting his grandmother. She chided herself—it wasn't *that* kind of meeting, as though he'd taken her home to meet his parents or something. But it was strange how circumstances had thrown them together since that first day on the trail.

Sure, they'd been initially forced together that day, but David had made the decision to stick with her since then, and though she'd tried to keep her heart out of it, she'd welcomed his help in all this. In fact, she wasn't sure what she would have done without his encouragement and support. His unwavering protective bearing. Besides, Tracy had kept herself so separate from everyone in Mountain Cove—except for Jewel—that she hadn't made any real friends.

Who was she kidding? She'd needed David these past few weeks. Needed him in a desperate way.

Katy stood in the kitchen making coffee. "David says you're interested in staying at the house. Renting a room. Only I won't accept that. You can stay with me for as long as you need without worrying about payment."

Tracy glanced at him, unsure what he'd told his grandmother. She was beginning to doubt this idea. How could she put this woman in danger like this? Anyone she got close to would be at risk. "Oh, no, I couldn't do that. I was considering renting the garage apartment."

And she was close to changing her mind on the whole arrangement. How had she let him talk her into this? It might be closer to town and in a neighborhood that felt more secure than being out in the woods in Jewel's cabin, but she'd been in a neighborhood when Santino had destroyed her life the first time.

She took a step back.

David blocked her way as if he'd read her mind.

"Grandma understands everything, Tracy. Don't worry." David winked at his grandmother. "In fact, she's been through this before."

"Besides," Katy said, "David is going to stay in the garage apartment. So you see? You have to stay in the house. It's a big lonely house with all the kids gone. I'd enjoy the company."

Tracy wasn't sure how good of company she would be. She felt a little cornered.

"You're staying in the apartment?"

"I am." His forest-eyed gaze pinned her, sending her heart tumbling.

"And Solomon's free to roam the house and the yard." Katy watched Tracy, waiting for her reaction. It was as if the woman was trying to persuade Tracy, too. How could anyone welcome someone in her situation into their home this way?

And how could Tracy say no to these two?

"My grandmother is the best cook, so at least eat dinner with us and then you can decide."

Oh, so he *had* read her mind.

"Make yourself comfortable, dear. Let David bring in your things." Katy grabbed her hand and dragged her forward, tossing a wink at David.

Tracy liked David's grandmother a lot.

Later that evening she settled into a bedroom upstairs, Solomon at her side. David and Katy and her amazing home-style cooking had worked against her, convincing her to stay when alarms had gone off in her head. But if not here, where would she stay? Anywhere else and she would be all alone and an easier target.

She didn't know how, but this family and this town made her feel more protected than she'd felt since this ordeal had first begun—when Derrick had started re-searching his story. Chief Winters had even stopped by the house to speak with her and reassure her they would keep an eye out with all vigilance.

But they couldn't go on like this forever. Though Tracy wanted this to end, she couldn't foresee any ending that wouldn't cost more lives.

Tracy woke at dawn when her SAR pager went off. She dug around in her backpack, realizing she'd almost for-gotten about the thing with everything that had happened.

She read the callout information. They needed Solo-mon for a wilderness search. A little girl was missing. Tracy couldn't abide that, couldn't sit around and do noth-ing. She'd moved to Mountain Cove to be free and she intended to live her life. Besides, she'd be with others on the search, and needed to get her mind off herself and onto others.

Solomon looked up at her, wagging his tail. He'd rec-ognized the sound and knew what it meant. Wondering if David had also received it, she peeked out the window. His truck was gone. That was right; he was at the fire station for his shift. He'd taken off far too much time on her account already, she was sure.

Tracy geared up and headed down the stairs. Katy was already up and drinking coffee, a deep frown etched in her face. What could that be about? Her eyes grew wide when she saw Tracy.

"Good morning, Tracy. You're up early for work."

"Not exactly. I don't start back helping Jewel until next

week." Tracy shrugged as she took the mug Katy poured her, feeling guilty and yet so grateful to Jewel for her understanding. Who could ask for a better employer? "I need to go now, though, because I received a callout. They need a SAR dog to find a little girl. She went missing this morning."

Katy nodded, her frown deepening. "There was a fire in town last night. I've been praying for David and the other firefighters, and for Adam. It was his business that burned."

Tracy stiffened, fear curdling in her stomach. She'd slept so hard she hadn't heard the sirens. And poor Adam. Had it been another attack related to Santino? A warning that hit closer to the Warren home, targeting David's family this time? Tracy prayed it wasn't related. Everything couldn't be because of her situation, could it? *God, please, no...* She composed herself. "Anyone hurt? Have you heard from David?"

"He said he would text when he could. I would have gone up there, but David wouldn't have it, and I didn't want to leave you here alone. But I believe that God holds my grandchildren in the palm of His hand. Who am I to worry? But instead I pray. Can I pray for you?"

Seeing the strength of those words in Katy's eyes, Tracy wished she had that same kind of faith. "Sure, you can pray. I'll pray, too. I'm so sorry for Adam."

She hung her head, not knowing how to express everything she felt. Then, finally, she said, "Thank you, again, for letting me stay. I should get going."

She wanted to see David and Adam, but knew she would only distract them. Besides, she and Solomon had a job to do. Something to help others.

To Solomon she said, "Come on, boy. We have work to do today. We have to help find a little girl who is lost."

EIGHTEEN

Tracy and Solomon were one of three dog teams deployed to different areas near where the family had camped. She wore a bright orange jacket, as did Solomon, so they could be easily spotted. Dog teams were the most effective first response in searching for a missing person, especially in this wilderness. Especially since it had started raining early this morning.

Solomon was a good air-scent dog, and the weather wouldn't keep him from locating someone, because the little girl would continue to emit a scent, and Solomon would find it. But that was the problem—he wasn't a tracking dog and couldn't tell people's scents apart. When he followed what he could tell was a human scent, it could be anyone. That was why they were on their own now, so Solomon would pick up only the little girl's scent. Her name was Emily and she was only ten years old.

Her parents had discovered her missing this morning. It was likely that she had left the tent sometime during the night while her parents were sleeping and somehow gotten lost. Tracy prayed for Emily and knew Katy and others would be praying, as well. For some reason, she felt as though Katy's prayers would surely be answered. The faith in that woman was palpable.

Following Solomon as he searched the wooded area, Tracy recalled when she and David had been searching for him in the woods, only to find him in the mining shaft. At least the undergrowth was thinned out here and easier to walk through. Easier to see. Maybe Emily had gone this way, since she wouldn't have had to work her way through the thick undergrowth and greenery. The thoughts sent her mind to David again.

She hoped David and the other firemen had extinguished the fire by now, but of course, the rain would help. She couldn't shake the feeling the fire was related to Santino, as well. She prayed it wasn't. Plenty went wrong in life that had nothing at all to do with Tracy and the man intent on retaliation.

But Tracy focused on the situation, shoving her own predicament out of her mind. At least for now. It felt good to think about someone else for a change.

After an hour searching, Tracy was surprised they hadn't found Emily yet. How could the girl have wandered so far? Tracy called Solomon back to give him water and take a break.

Her radio squawked. Tracy answered.

"Emily is alive and well!"

"Oh, thank the Lord." Tracy sighed in relief. She leaned against a tree and took a swig of water. "You hear that, Solomon? We can head back now."

The rain had eased up to a trickle.

A sound startled her. A spattering of leaves. A *thunk* of something hitting a tree behind her head. Tracy froze, her mind slowly comprehending…

A bullet.

Then another bullet whizzed by her and hit the tree a few feet away.

She ducked for cover behind the tree, holding Solomon

to her. She wasn't sure if Solomon would be safer on his own, since Tracy was the obvious target, but she wasn't about to risk him out in the open when there were bullets flying. She wished they'd been in a thicker part of the woods and then she'd be harder to spot.

Tracy got on her radio. "Get everyone out. There's a shooter up here. He's taking shots at me!" She relayed her location.

"Are you all right?" Cade's voice came over the radio.

"Just…make sure everyone gets away." She choked back sobs and fear. She couldn't believe she'd actually put everyone in danger on a search and rescue. But for the life of her, she hadn't imagined this outcome.

"Get down and stay hidden."

She was glad the sniper wasn't a good shot or she would already be dead. But maybe that was the point— to drag it out so as to torture her before he killed her. She pressed her face into her hands.

"Oh, God, please, help me! Please keep others safe. I need this to end."

The tree next to her took a beating. She needed to get out of her bright-colored jacket, but instead she was forced to slink even lower onto the ground, into the spruce needles and ferns, pressing Solomon down beside her. He whined and barked, understanding she was in distress.

"Shh." She comforted him. He couldn't understand their dangerous situation.

But she'd protect him. He'd been the one to save her that awful night, but now she faced a new threat by the same man. This was it, then. If she survived this, she would get a new identity and leave her family behind. Maybe they could fake her funeral so all attempts at retaliation would stop. She wasn't indecisive anymore. This had to stop.

She'd thought that either she or Santino had to die, and now she knew. That was the only way. She had to die.

But not today!

Another bullet whizzed by, taunting her. Tracy removed her jacket and Solomon's, then crawled away from them while she tried to maintain the protection of the trees.

Sweat slid down her temples and back. At any moment a bullet could blast through her skull. Though a fierce will to survive rose up in her, tears slid down her cheeks. Almost nothing she'd experienced so far could compare to the terror she felt right now. Each incident seemed to increasingly terrify her until she knew she couldn't take any more.

Flat on the ground, she crawled, the foliage scratching her. Insects scuttled over her and mosquitoes buzzed in her ear. She remained still as best she could and listened, waiting for the next shot. Solomon grew antsy, but she pressed him next to her.

"There now, you're a good dog," she said, twisting her fingers through his fur to calm him.

Another bullet slammed a tree much too close. So taking off her jacket hadn't thrown the shooter off. She was a dead woman if help didn't come soon. They knew she was in trouble, but how could they get to her in time? How could the police find her exact location without endangering themselves?

Any rescue would mean taking out the sniper first.

Solomon growled and bolted from her grasp.

"Solomon! No!"

Next she heard him yelp. Her pulse jumped as she peered through the foliage. Whimpering, Solomon lay still.

Gasping for breath, David ran through the woods. Pushing off trunks. Jumping a brook. The movements reminded him of the day they'd found Jay. Solomon had sounded off and David had known something was wrong. He'd run through the woods, looking for Tracy. He hadn't known then what he knew now.

Someone wanted her dead.

He wanted to call her name. Shout out for her. But a sniper was shooting at Tracy, and he couldn't call attention to either of them. If she had remained at the coordinates she'd given Cade, he knew exactly where she was.

Rotor blades thumped in the distance. Winters had already called the Alaska State Troopers to help. Mountain Cove police were preparing to move in to catch the sniper. But none of them were moving fast enough, as far as David was concerned.

He heard the sound of the suppressed rifle and the ping against trees. How much ammo had this guy brought with him? And how many shots would he take before he hit Tracy? He either wasn't much of a sniper or was toying with her. Or maybe the thick forest had protected her. The forest and God. But David was getting close to her. He pressed his back against a trunk.

"Tracy, can you hear me?" He kept his voice low so it wouldn't carry too far.

Let her be okay, God.

He banked on the fact that the sniper continued shooting meant she was still alive.

"Tracy, are you there?" *Please, be there.*

A bullet hit the tree near David's head. Compared to everything that had happened so far, a sniper in the woods brought everything to a whole new level. City gangs tended to prefer their hits up close and personal—their ranks wouldn't include a trained sniper. Was this a soldier who'd become corrupted, hired by the gang, or a gang member who'd gotten his training somewhere? David slipped behind another tree trunk, moving closer to the sniper's target area, and slid to the ground. He didn't know what he would do if something happened to Tracy.

Then he heard it.

Quiet sobbing.

David peered around the tree, close to the ground, hoping the troopers in the helicopter would get the sniper or at least distract him. Crawling forward, he peered through the foliage and thought he saw her just through the thicket.

"Tracy." Louder this time.

"David?" Her voice was choked with tears.

But hearing her ignited hope in him. "I'm here. Stay there—I'm coming to you."

"No! I don't want you to get killed!"

David ignored her and crawled forward until he found her leaning over Solomon. The dog had been shot. Grief squeezed his gut. He closed the distance and pulled Tracy to him. Trembling, she sobbed in his shoulder.

"It isn't safe for us to stay. I have to get you out of here."

"I won't leave Solomon. He's still alive."

"The police and troopers are closing in on the sniper. Maybe that will give us the chance we need."

She vigorously shook her head. "He could have killed me already. He's just playing with me. Torturing me before the end. That's why he shot Solomon. We can't wait here for him to die. I would have carried him out myself if I could have."

In the distance they heard a voice blasting over a megaphone, telling the gunman to give it up.

More gunfire ensued. An exchange between the police and the sniper?

If they'd engaged him, David could carry Solomon out now. The dog wouldn't make it if he didn't get medical attention soon.

He peered through the tree crowns and in the distance saw the men lowering from the helicopter into the woods. Had they caught the sniper?

David got on Tracy's radio to the ICC. "What's the news?"

"They got him," the dispatcher at the Incident Command Center reported.

"We're coming in," he said. "I'm carrying Solomon. He's been shot."

Carefully he lifted Solomon. "Let's keep to the trees as much as possible. In case he wasn't alone."

He hoped he wasn't making a mistake, but they couldn't stay here and watch Solomon die.

Together they trekked through the woods, David hurrying as fast as he could, careful not to hurt Solomon more and conscious that every second counted in getting the dog the help he needed. Still, David couldn't help but be glad it wasn't an injured Tracy that he carried now.

After a couple of miles, sweat was like a second skin on him, even though he was in Alaska. Behind him, Tracy stumbled.

He paused and turned, prepared to help her up. "Are you okay?"

Her expression more distraught than he'd ever seen, she nodded. "I'm okay. Keep going. Get Solomon help. I'll catch up if I have to."

He wouldn't argue with her, but if she slipped too far behind, David would slow and wait. She might disagree with him, but her safety was still his priority.

"Just hold on, Solomon." He knew the dog meant everything to her, especially since he had saved her life.

David had yet to hear the full story even though they'd spent ample time together traveling to and from Missouri. He understood her reticence well enough—she didn't want to talk about that night. It was something she wanted to forget even while she went through retaliation for being the witness to put Santino in prison.

Winters appeared in his vision in the distance and jogged toward him. He reached for the dog. "Let me help."

"I've got him," David said. "Call the vet—Harrison—for me. I'm heading to his office now."

"Already done," Winters said.

Tracy followed David to the new truck he'd bought in Juneau and parked at the trailhead. She opened the door and got in, and David placed Solomon in her lap. The grief constricting his chest matched the fear and sorrow written across her face. Her gaze locked with his.

Would they lose Solomon?

Not on his watch. Not if he could help it.

He ran around to the driver's side and threw out questions to Winters. "Is he still alive? Can you question him? Put an end to this?"

A dark shadow fell across the police chief's face. "No. Take care of the dog and Tracy. I'll check in with you later. Maybe I'll know more by then. But we need to talk soon."

David burned rubber, headed toward town. He'd gone nuts when he'd come back from putting out the fire that took down Adam's bike shop. That had been bad enough, but then he'd learned that Tracy had been targeted by a sniper while she was out on a search. He hadn't had a moment to think through any of that, but now all his frustration came rushing in. What had she been thinking? What had *anyone* been thinking to let her go out on her own like that?

God help him, he couldn't live without her, and yet, apparently, he couldn't live with her, either, because she wouldn't be allowed to live. Not this way. But he would bring none of that up now. It wasn't the time.

He risked a glance in her direction, reining in his emotions and anything he might say. Tears brimmed in her eyes. The way she looked at him, he could swear he saw feelings for him in her eyes. And though he'd denied it for so long, if he let himself be honest, he loved her, too. But as God would have it, he would lose a woman he loved—again.

NINETEEN

Tracy cradled Solomon, fearing his life was seeping out of him with every passing minute. She held tight as David raced down the road, passing cars, even receiving a few honks, and steered into the small parking space at the veterinarian's office. Chief Winters was supposed to tell the vet to expect them, and she hoped he was available to deal with this emergency right away.

And it was an emergency. She couldn't lose Solomon.

David opened her door and reached for her dog. He carried Solomon to the door, David's long legs making strides she couldn't keep up with. Someone was there waiting and opened the door for him.

Once they were inside, the tall, lanky vet opened the door to his operating room. Relief swelled in Tracy—he'd been ready and waiting to save her search-and-rescue dog. Solomon had saved lives. He deserved this. David laid the dog on the table and nodded at the vet, his expression conveying he trusted the man to save Solomon.

His efforts and concern for her dog broke through her grief. David ushered her out of the room and closed the door behind him. "Let him do his job and we'll do ours."

Tears swelled but they didn't fall. Not yet. She didn't

think she could cry any more and didn't want to. "What's our job, David?"

"Pray. We're going to sit here and pray."

The past few hours crashed in on her and sent her into a daze. She took the seat next to David and let him hold her hand. He started praying, but her mind kept drifting to images of David trekking through the woods, holding Solomon. The dog had saved her from the flames. But fire had taken Derrick's life for the investigative reporting he was doing on Santino's gang. Three long years later and she was still in this nightmare, orchestrated by the same man.

David squeezed her hand and continued his soft prayer, then slipped into a silence of his own. She'd never forget the way he'd carried Solomon through the woods, undaunted against all obstacles, as though his own life depended on it. The title "hero" didn't begin to describe this man sitting next to her. Or what he meant to her.

Tracy finally realized there were others sitting in the waiting room with their pets. And they were wide-eyed as they looked at David and Tracy.

David squeezed her hand. "He's going to be okay, Tracy. You have to believe that."

"Can we go outside for some fresh air?"

"Sure." He got up and led her out the door.

They walked around to the side of the building facing the woods.

David lifted her chin, forcing her to look at him. A tangle of emotions emanated from his gaze. "Are you hurt? In all the rush to save Solomon, I failed to ask you."

"I'm fine. Not even a bullet graze this time. Which is why I don't get any of this. Does Santino want to kill me or not? Or is he laughing from his prison cell while he attacks everyone around me? I think…I think he enjoys letting me know that he can get to me if he wants to. And once I'm dead, the fun will be over for him. What I never understood is how he found me."

"Come here." David pulled her into his arms. "Winters said he would call me with more information. But the shooter is dead, at least. It's over."

Tracy clung to David. She soaked up his reassurances and strength, wanting to believe those words with everything in her. For today, they were enough to get her through. She'd wait until Solomon was strong enough and then she must make the ultimate sacrifice. She never dreamed she'd be in this position, but she would have to leave this man.

A man she loved.

A man she couldn't love—it would cost him his life.

"David? Tracy?" The veterinarian's assistant stood a few feet away.

David released Tracy.

"Yes?" they said together.

"Solomon is out of surgery. We removed the bullet and he's going to be fine. We need to keep him a few days."

"Yes, whatever he needs, do it." The tears chose that moment to spill. Tracy wiped at them furiously. "Can I see him?"

Tracy and David followed the petite blonde into the room where they kept Solomon. Tracy pressed her hand on his head and wound her fingers through his fur. Asleep, he couldn't respond.

"That was much too close," she said.

She glanced up at the vet, respecting his time and that he had other patients to attend to. "Will he be able to return to work as a search-and-rescue dog?"

The man frowned, uncertainty carved in his features. "It's too early to say. We removed the bullet, but the penetrating trauma collapsed his lung. We had to insert a chest tube until his lung heals."

"And how long will that be?"

"Days before we remove the tube. Weeks before he's completely healed. As far as him returning as a work dog, only time will tell. If you'll excuse me, I need to get to my other patients."

"Of course." Tracy forced a smile and thrust out her hand to shake his. "Thank you for saving him."

"Always my pleasure." He exited the room.

When he was gone, Tracy's knees grew weak. She pressed her face into her hands. "How can I ever love anyone, if my family, friends, someone I meet at the grocery store, if even my dog isn't safe?"

David's cell buzzed in his pocket.

Wanting to comfort Tracy, he ignored the call and tugged her to him. He was still running on the adrenaline that had carried him through the woods to find her and then had sustained him as he'd brought Solomon back and rushed him to the veterinarian. But he inhaled a deep breath, bracing for the expected crash.

He held on to her, knowing she would leave Mountain Cove as soon as Solomon recovered enough to travel. She could never leave her dog behind. But she would leave David and her family behind. And he'd never see her again. There was no way she could stay. She'd tried to make it work. They both had. But they were no match for Santino and his resources.

His cell buzzed again. Must be something important.

Tracy pulled from his arms. She wiped at her eyes and looked at him. "We need to get out of here, and you need to answer your phone."

David followed her out as he tugged the phone from his pocket. Chief Winters.

David answered the call.

"Where are you?" Winters asked.

"At the vet's office. Solomon will live. But he'll be here for a few days and won't fully recover for a few weeks."

"Good. Now, listen. Get her out of there."

"What?" David kept his voice low as they walked through the lobby. He opened the door for Tracy and they stepped outside.

"Take Tracy and leave Mountain Cove. Don't stop to get anything." His tone was urgent.

David eyed Tracy, who watched him intently. "Hold on," he said into the phone. He unlocked his truck and opened the door for Tracy. Still watching him, she climbed inside.

Once he'd closed the door, he continued his conversation with Winters as he walked around to the driver's side. "What's going on, Winters? Tracy is going into WITSEC after this. She'll be leaving Mountain Cove as soon as Solomon heals."

"I'm not sure that's good enough at this point. Or fast enough. I have my suspicions. I'm following a lead, and I don't want to say anything until I know more, but drive to the floatplane dock and catch the next flight out. Take a boat. I don't care. Just get her out."

David stood by his door, but didn't open it. Tracy eyed him from inside the truck. The police chief was telling him that Mountain Cove police couldn't protect her. "Where am I supposed to take her?"

"I don't care. But don't tell anyone your plans." Voices resounded in the background. "Listen, I don't have time to say more, but I'll be in touch as soon as I can." Winters ended the call.

David stared at his phone. What was going on? And what was he supposed to tell Tracy? She wouldn't want to leave without Solomon. He climbed into the truck and avoided her gaze.

"What was that about?"

"I don't know. I'm still trying to figure it out." He ran both hands through his hair. Puffed his cheeks and blew out a breath. He needed a plan and fast.

Tracy sighed and stared out the window. Her thoughts were clearly on Solomon's injuries and what she'd just endured. "You know what this means, don't you?"

"Tell me." David started his truck and steered from the parking lot. He suspected he knew what she was going to say, but what Winters had said to him, which wasn't much, changed everything. Deep down he'd mentally prepared for the moment when she would say goodbye to him forever. And maybe that moment would come. But not yet.

"Nothing you don't already know. This is it, David. I can't take this anymore. They hurt my father and now Solomon. I have to go. Maybe the marshals can just fake my death. Have a funeral and this can all be over for everyone I love. This won't end until Santino thinks I'm dead. I have to wait for Solomon to get strong, though. I knew this would happen, I just…I just hoped it wouldn't come to this."

She was right. He already knew, but he'd hoped as she had. And there was more going on than either of them knew about. David steered toward downtown.

"I know they were supposed to move Santino into isolation," he said. He needed time to figure out how to tell her his plans. "Or away from the prison gangs. They were looking at options to keep him from directing his retaliation. But clearly that isn't working."

"It's just a matter of time before someone else gets hurt." The intensity in her gaze let him know the words had double meaning. She was worried about *him* getting hurt.

Didn't she know it was too late? Her leaving him would leave a long, painful gash in his heart. Yeah, the one he'd protected so well. Though he'd known all along, that hadn't prevented him from taking this fall. But he was going with her now, taking her out of Mountain Cove. How would she feel about that? And what if…what if he went into WITSEC with her? Was that even an option? He hadn't seriously considered that before. He had family here that counted on him. He understood Tracy's turmoil and why she had refused to consider leaving her family before now.

He'd spent almost a decade trying to figure out why God would let Natalie die in that fire. Though he might not ever get the answer to that question, he had a feeling that God was giving him a second chance at love but David had to choose to take it.

He turned off Main Street and headed to the floatplane dock, hoping he could get a ride on something to somewhere. Hoping he could convince Tracy to come with him. That would be the hardest part. He'd call one of his brothers and get them to move his truck. Didn't need anyone figuring out they'd gone too soon.

He turned into the parking lot near the seaplane dock and parked. As if only now realizing where they were, Tracy sat taller. Took in a breath.

"What are we doing here? I thought we were heading…home." She frowned.

Was that her choice of words? Calling his grandmother's house "home"? He liked that. But they might never see this place again.

And, yeah, he was in it for the long haul if she'd let him. That reality slapped him dizzy.

David turned to face her and leaned closer. "That was Chief Winters on the phone a few minutes ago. He said you need to leave now. Don't pass go. Don't collect two hundred dollars."

Her eyes widened. "But I can't leave. What about Solomon?"

"Solomon will be fine. My family will care for him until we get back."

"We?"

"Yes. I'm going with you. We're leaving now."

She frantically shook her head. "I don't understand. What's going on?"

David climbed out of the truck and opened her door, assisting her. She appeared stunned. Why hadn't she been prepared to be instantly whisked away? Wasn't that how the marshals protected witnesses? Maybe she'd gotten accustomed to the pace she'd had in Mountain Cove. Regardless, things had escalated.

"I have no idea, but he said he would call me. It sounded like he'd come across some information he needed to check into. But I've never heard him sound so urgent. I trust him."

"I need to call Jennifer and have her take care of things from her end."

David spotted Billy. "And you'll get your chance. Winters didn't think we had time for that just now. Priority one needs to be getting away from here."

"Where are we going?"

"Just trust me, will you?" He was making this up as he went. But David had already thought of friends he knew in the Seward area. He'd spent a lot of time on the Kenai Peninsula fighting fires. From there, they could take the

Alaska Railroad or drive into Anchorage. There were a lot more options. More places to hide in Interior Alaska. More ways to get in and out.

Let Santino find her there.

He'd have to go through David if he did.

TWENTY

Tracy was on the ride of her life.

Or at least it felt that way as she disembarked from the plane at Seward with only the clothes on her back. And no Solomon. David came up behind her, wrapped his arm around her waist and ushered her forward.

She'd left her bright orange jacket in the forest, and now she shivered. It was colder here.

She'd never felt so lost in her life. "So it's come to this. I'm literally looking over my shoulder to watch for someone trying to kill me as I run and hide."

Disquiet surfaced in his gaze. And this man—she swallowed the lump in her throat—this man had chosen to go with her. But she couldn't let him do that. At least not all the way. She couldn't allow him to disappear with her for good. That was asking too much. Yet at this moment, she had no choice but to stay close to him. He was the one who knew where they were going for now.

"What next?" she asked.

"I contact my friends. See if there's someplace we can stay tonight while we figure things out. At least we're out of Mountain Cove. At least you're safe. No one knows I have friends here. No one will think to look for you here."

As if that had mattered before.

"And I need to get us transportation."

He riffled through a thick wad of bills he'd pulled from his pocket. Nausea roiled in her gut. Did he normally keep such a large amount of cash on him?

"David, I can't let you pay for all this." Then again, she was close to running out of money. She couldn't sustain this kind of life—staying on the move to stay alive—for very long. Not without turning to her family for money they couldn't easily spare, on top of the medical bills and the cost of beefing up their home security.

Oh, Lord, when will this ever end?

He eyed her then pulled out some twenties. "This is a matter of life and death, Tracy. Let's find a place to stay. I'll call Chief Winters to find out more about what is going on. But the important thing is your safety."

Tracy nodded and let David take the lead. He knew what he was doing in this part of the world. Tracy didn't have a clue where they were other than a name on a map.

An hour and a half later she was sitting in the kitchen of a cozy log cabin just outside of the small town, getting acquainted with David's friends—an older couple named John and Kari Nash, who eagerly welcomed them into their home.

Of course they could stay for as long as they needed.

Of course they had plenty of space and Tracy would have her separate room. The couple was old-fashioned that way. Besides, Tracy and David weren't a couple.

Were they?

David settled into an easy conversation with them about the local wildfire threat. She'd known he was a firefighter in Mountain Cove, but was stunned to hear of his extensive experience fighting wildland fires all over the region. Stunned to realize how much time she'd spent with the man lately and how little she really knew him. But that was just as well. Her life was not her own, she finally realized.

Her head was spinning with all that had happened within a few hours. She'd been all set to tell David goodbye, to say goodbye to everyone including her family, but today she'd said that word to no one. And she'd left Solomon behind, something she would never have willingly done.

John took David outside to show him something and left Tracy alone with Kari. The woman showed her the cozy room upstairs decorated in the same country style as Jewel's cottage, which made her feel more at home. As though she could breathe for the first time in weeks. Kari found Tracy some extra clothing, including a coat. Tracy hadn't exactly come prepared. After she took a long, hot bath and changed into comfortable, warm sweats, she sneaked downstairs to see if she could catch David. She needed to know what was going on and hoped he'd talked to Chief Winters again by now. But he wasn't there. The lights were out in the house except for the fire in the fireplace. Daylight waned outside, but it would be hours before dark.

Tracy crept back to her room and called Jennifer to let her know she needed a new life and fast. The thing was, she'd have to leave Solomon until someone could bring him to her. As usual, she left a voice mail. Through the window she spotted David and John exiting the barn and assumed they were heading back to the house, until John got in his vehicle and drove off.

Tracy went downstairs to wait for David. When he didn't immediately come inside, she moved to the sofa near the fire, glad for the warmth.

When David finally came inside he made for the stairs and then paused when he spotted her. "I didn't see you."

"I've been waiting for you."

He moved to the sofa and sat next to her, but not too close. "Sorry. Had some catching up to do with John. And I had to call Chief Winters."

"And?"

"I didn't get through, but left a message. He'll call me back. Don't worry."

"And then what, David?"

He leaned back on the sofa and reached over. Twisted her hair around his finger. "We do whatever we have to do to keep you safe."

"I appreciate all you've done for me. But I can't let you go any further."

Sitting here next to him in the soft firelight, she saw in his eyes the hurt she'd wanted to avoid, the same hurt she felt inside. But they were both adults, both knew they shouldn't get involved. She realized she wanted much more with him, but life had been so unfair.

Tracy couldn't help herself. She tilted forward and gently pressed her lips against his. "You said you'd never kiss me again, I know. But I'm kissing you now."

She slipped her hands around his neck and pulled him closer. David responded as she knew he would and enclosed her in his arms, deepening his kiss. Their kiss was filled with regret and longing and a forbidden love that neither could afford. Deep down, she knew this fireman hero in a way she'd never known Derrick, a man she'd once hoped to marry.

And here she was, letting Santino destroy her life again. But he'd taken so much more than her existence—he'd killed people, hurt them in devastating ways, all because of his need for retaliation against her testimony that had put him away. The pain and memories jarred into her emotions.

David gently eased from her lips. "What's wrong?" His voice was husky, filled with the passion of the moment.

She leaned her forehead against him. "It's not you, David. It's that in the end I'm letting Santino destroy my life. I'm going to run and hide. I'm going to disappear."

He tipped her chin up so she'd look at him. "You never told me what happened."

He definitely deserved to hear the story before she left.

David wrapped his arms around her as they both stared into the fire and she spilled everything she'd kept pent up inside. She'd wanted to forget that night, but apparently she couldn't leave her past behind her.

"I loved a man I worked with at the newspaper. We had talked of marriage, and I'd hoped he would pop the question soon. But he'd wanted to finish the dangerous project he was working on first.

"Derrick was an investigative reporter digging into Santino's gang and their crimes, including the recent arsons that had set the city on fire. The people that died. None of it typical of gangs, and Santino wasn't even a suspect until Derrick dug deeper. He'd received death threats, and then when I started getting them, Derrick was prepared to back out. But I convinced him to keep going. I believe in doing the right thing and not letting criminals win the day. Me... I'm the reason."

Tracy burst into tears and kept crying until they were spent. David sat next to her. He didn't say a word, just waited patiently for her to finish. He understood what she needed—not judgment or platitudes, but for him to simply listen.

"Solomon jumped on the bed, barking at me—that's what woke me. Flames engulfed my house. I was tied up in my bed. Apparently, I'd been drugged. Solomon had been locked away, but he'd clawed his way free. I barely got the two of us out before succumbing to the smoke and flames. But before I passed out, I saw Santino himself and a few others, dousing the house next door with accelerant. He was definitely a pyromaniac. But Derrick? He hadn't been so fortunate. He didn't have Solomon to pull him from a drugged stupor. His house—on the other side of town—burned down with him inside… like the other victims."

David held and comforted her, and Tracy allowed herself to fully release her anguish for the first time since this had all begun. There'd been no one who could comfort her before, not even her family. But this man next to her had already been through much of this with her in recent days, and he understood her as no one else could.

She wiped her eyes. "How many times have I cried on your shoulder?"

"I don't know. A couple hundred?"

She gently rapped him. "I hope you understand now. I want to care about you, but I can't afford to. I can't stand by any longer while people, even animals, I care about get hurt. I wanted to stand strong like my father, but I'm not doing him any favors by hanging on to this life in Mountain Cove. A life I've grown to love. People…" She leaned her forehead against his chin. "People I've grown to love."

She wouldn't say the actual words directed to him. Saying it would mean letting it happen, and she couldn't do that to either of them—not when she was leaving. "I've given myself tonight to say goodbye. I'm leaving as soon as the marshal can get here."

Surprise rocked through David.

He shoved up from the couch. "You called her?"

She nodded. "I didn't reach her. I never do. But I left her all the pertinent information."

David scraped his hands through his hair and paced in front of the fire. Winters had said not to tell *anyone*. Could he have meant Marshal Hanes, too?

"Why didn't you wait until I talked to Winters?"

"What's the point, David? We know I have to leave."

David sat on the edge of the sofa, next to her again. "The thing is…" This wasn't exactly how he'd planned to broach the subject. It wasn't romantic. And the timing was just all wrong.

Goodbye…

He couldn't let her say that word to him. Yet if he deserved a second chance, how did he convince her to let him disappear with her, too? But his family here needed him, as well. David was more torn than ever.

"Tracy," he whispered. Overcome with what he felt for her, he kissed her again, pushing that one word— *goodbye*—out of his mind. Yet it hovered at the edge, nonetheless.

In her kisses he understood what she would not say to him. Understood what he couldn't say to her. He wished this evening wouldn't end, that tomorrow would never come. At the same time, he knew he couldn't hide anything from her anymore.

Before he lost complete control he pulled back and then kissed her on the forehead. He needed to tell her everything.

"My wife died in a fire, Tracy. So I understand how you feel. You blame yourself, when you couldn't have done anything to stop it. But in my case, I'm a fireman. There's no reason that my wife should have died in our house. It shouldn't have burned down. I shouldn't have left her. I promised her I'd be back.

"But back then I traveled all over Alaska or the Pacific Northwest, wherever wildland firefighters were needed.

I was gone for long stretches at a time. She begged me to stay, but I was too pigheaded to listen. I did what I wanted to do. Every time I left, she was afraid I wouldn't come back. I was off saving someone else and while the most important person in my life needed me at home. The night the fire burned down our house, I'd come here, to the Kenai Peninsula to fight a wildfire."

David squeezed his eyes shut. He couldn't bear to think that she had suffered or called for him, but the way he understood it, she'd died in her sleep from smoke inhalation. "I didn't know it, but she had a prescription for sleeping pills. She couldn't sleep for worry when I was gone and that's why she hadn't responded to the smoke alarm in the house. So at the end of the day, I'm to blame for her death."

"You can't blame yourself for that. That was her decision."

"How can I not? Everyone has regrets in life and that's mine. I wish I could go back and change what happened. Second chances don't always come in this life. I didn't feel I deserved a second chance, but God gave me the start of one with you anyway. And even if it all ends tonight, I'll always be grateful for that—grateful that through this hard time, I got to be the one who was there for you, who helped you through it all."

With his words he kissed Tracy again. Eventually, Tracy ended their kiss. Her frown deepening, he saw jumbled emotions spill from her eyes. She scraped her hands through her luscious red hair and David was glad he'd at least had the privilege to run his fingers through it, and to kiss her, though he wasn't sure that had been fair to either of their hearts.

"If there was a way for me to stay, I would. You know that."

"I do." And then what? It wouldn't be safe for her. And he couldn't ask her to put herself at risk for his sake. "I think I've known from the beginning, when you first told me the truth, it would end this way."

Unless Santino died. Or Tracy did.

TWENTY-ONE

Tracy pressed her back against the bedroom door. David had left. Walked out of the house when they'd heard John's vehicle return. Somehow she'd thought their conversation would go much differently. It hadn't gone the way she'd wanted but her life wasn't going the way she wanted.

David Warren.

Just a few short weeks ago that name had conjured much different thoughts of the man.

But now? She'd loved his tender kisses and everything about him. And nothing could ever come of it.

She made a phone call to Jennifer again, this time finally getting the marshal instead of voice mail. Carlos Santino was being moved, Jennifer assured Tracy, and she should be relatively safe. But there was no assurance there would not be future incidents. The only guarantee would come when Tracy Murray disappeared and became someone else in a new life and a new place. Tracy was instructed to stay where she was until the marshals came for her.

This time, Tracy would take the deal.

She bit back tears and managed to work her way through the rest of the conversation. Time was running out. Tracy Murray would have to die.

This was the first night she'd spent alone since she'd

first gotten the puppy she'd named Solomon, after King Solomon. The way his golden fur had crowned his head, she'd thought the name fitting. And since that night he'd saved her, she could sleep easier knowing he was with her. But tonight, she felt numb all over and didn't think she could sleep for thinking about her nebulous future that would include none of the people she loved. At least Solomon would go with her.

Her heart twisted and nausea roiled in her stomach at the thought of leaving everyone behind. According to Jennifer, she would at least have the opportunity to say one last goodbye.

She stared at the ceiling for hours until she fell into a fitful sleep.

Coughing...

Tracy woke to incessant coughing. Smoke alarms screamed. Where was she? Where was Solomon? Why wasn't he barking, waking her up as the room filled with smoke and the smell of fire?

No. This was definitely not a dream. And she didn't think her faked death would come like this.

She made for the door as smoke and heat wrapped around her, sending her into a panic.

Oh, God, no. Not again!

Her eyes burned; she couldn't see. She squeezed them shut, mind racing with thoughts of how to get out of here, get free of the flames. Strong arms wrapped around her and she knew right away that they weren't David's. There was cruelty and hatred in the tight, bruising grip.

She opened her eyes and Santino stared at her, an evil grin on his tattoo-riddled face.

Tracy tried to scream but he covered her mouth with tape. She couldn't cough, couldn't breathe. Darkness edged her vision. With what little strength she had left, she fought for freedom but his grip only tightened. He whisked her down a ladder at the back of the house and then, at the bottom, threw her over his shoulder in a fireman's carry.

Then everything went black.

Tracy woke coughing again. The tape had been removed from her mouth so she could breathe in the fresh air; only the scent of smoke still hung in the air, in her nostrils. She was bound to a tree, the setup sending her back to that night in her house. Solomon had saved her.

He hadn't been there to save her tonight, and in an odd twist, Santino had been the one to carry her out of the house. Why had he done that? Where was David? "Where am I?"

Santino might have carried her out of the house, but he'd started the fire. There could be no doubt there. And he hadn't saved her. He was the one bent on killing her. But what of the others in the house?

God, please keep David and his friends safe.

Footfalls crunched on spruce needles behind her. She stiffened. Santino walked around to stand in front of her, that sinister grin leering at her. "This time your dog won't save you. But I'm hoping your new boyfriend will come for you. That is, if he survives the fire."

"No! You're crazy, the worst kind of evil. David!" She tried to break free as she called his name.

God, please let him live.

She wanted to pray that David would find and save her, but she couldn't pray that. She couldn't be that selfish. It was enough for David to survive. She didn't want him to risk his life for her. She couldn't be the reason he died.

"What are you going to do to me?"

Santino gestured to the lights coming off Seward in the distance. "Let's see what happens when the forest that surrounds the town where you thought you could hide this time goes up in flames. Your boyfriend thought he was so smart, taking you away, but it didn't work. You can never escape." He stuck his face in hers. "I'm going to enjoy watching the look on your face when I set your world on fire."

Santino walked away from her until she could see only his silhouette. What was he doing? Looked as though, sounded as though he was pouring something from a canister.

Accelerant.

She closed her eyes. This was what she'd seen that night. This was her nightmare all over again.

God, how could this happen? How can You let this happen?

But she understood too well that giving people free will meant allowing evil in the world. That was what the criminal-justice system was for. How had Santino escaped? How had he found her so quickly? The obvious answer snaked around her neck and choked her. She jerked against the rope as though she could free herself. No, no, no, no. She didn't want to die this way.

To die the way Derrick had.

Even in the darkness, she thought she could see Santino's evil grin as he dropped a match. Flames erupted behind him. He strode toward her, a wall of fire quickly spreading behind him, cutting her off from the town and any possible rescue.

"See you on the other side of this life," he said as he walked past her.

If only Tracy had gone into WITSEC from the beginning, then none of this would be happening. David would be safe at home. John and Kari's home wouldn't be burning, and the forest wouldn't be ablaze.

How could she have made such a colossal mistake? Cost more lives?

Tracy prayed for her life and for the lives of others. The fire spread out hard and fast against the dry foliage of summer. Flames inched toward her, as well. Thankfully the wind was blowing away from her. Maybe Santino had planned it that way so she could suffer longer. She didn't know. But the wind could shift at any moment and then she would be consumed.

Now she understood why she hadn't been killed before now. He'd wanted to kill her himself. He'd wanted the chance to set her on fire.

The bright orange and yellow flames licked the sky, illuminating the area near Tracy. Behind the blaze, the sky was black with smoke in the thick of night. Surely firefighters would see and respond. If they weren't already busy putting out the fire at the house.

Squeezing her eyes shut, Tracy hung her head, the last of her prayers slipping from her heart. Nobody could save her this time.

Adrenaline coursing through his veins, David raced toward the wall of fire, his lungs burning from smoke and exertion.

He'd seen a man carry Tracy away from the house and into the woods, but he'd been trapped and couldn't get out in time to stop him. John had been the one to free David. He and Kari were safely out of the house.

He'd told John. He'd told him everything about the danger he and his wife would be facing if they allowed him and Tracy to stay with them, but the man had still wanted them to stay.

Fire trucks were on their way. The firefighters would save as much of the house as they could. He didn't have time to explain to anyone that he had to get to Tracy before someone killed her.

And when he'd looked into the darkness of a short Alaskan night, he'd seen the very instant the ground had been torched. Tracy had to be there. She had to be on the other side of the growing wall of fire. And David had to save her—he *had* to succeed in saving the woman he loved this time. He couldn't live with any other outcome.

But to see those flames licking this part of the world again—he'd been here nearly ten years before and the memory crushed the breath from him.

He raced toward the fire and fought his way through the thick, dry underbrush, racing the flames that blazed up the trees and into the crowns. He had to beat the fire, get to the other side before it spread and blocked his path to Tracy. Firefighters had to have seen the fire by now, but he wasn't sure they had the resources to battle it without calling in help. He'd been part of that help years ago. This wildland fire could blaze out of control before the required resources could be brought in.

What he wouldn't give to be wearing his firefighting gear at this moment.

God, please let me find her. She has to be here.

This was Santino's plan.

"Tracy! Where are you?"

"Here, I'm over here." Tracy's voice barely rose above the crackling roar of a growing wildfire.

David couldn't believe he'd heard her. The flames illuminated the woods, and in the distance, he spotted her tied to a tree. Anger burned in his gut. But he'd found her in time—hope burst through, infusing him with energy. He would beat the flames and save her.

The fire was growing dangerously close and heat licked his limbs. When he made it to Tracy, he slid to his knees, took out his pocketknife and cut the rope. He couldn't catch his breath enough to talk, but he doubted she could talk, either, if not from the stifling heat and choking smoke then from the shock evident on her face. Reflecting in her grateful eyes.

"It's Carlos Santino. He escaped. He's here." Her eyes grew wide. "David, behind you! It's Santino!"

David jerked around and jumped to his feet, prepared to fight.

A sneering man with a face covered in tattoos laughed in reply. "You came for her, like I knew you would."

Why did the man care if David had come for her? But David didn't need to know the answer to that.

"Tracy, get out of here." Anger boiling over, he lunged at the man.

They fought, and as the blows came, David knew he was no match for the man in terms of muscle and sheer strength. A man who'd been training for this moment in prison. But David had something Santino didn't have—the gut-wrenching determination to free the women he loved once and for all.

David had him in a headlock, but Santino escaped his grip and David saw the fear in his eyes—a haunting look David would never forget.

To his surprise, Santino turned and fled, running toward the flames. With Tracy's cries in his ears, he ran after him. He couldn't let him get away. Tracy would never be free if Santino escaped.

Unfortunately, even when he went back to prison, Tracy would never be free of Santino's grasp.

Tracy screamed, calling after David.

She couldn't believe it. Had she just seen David and Santino disappear through the fire? There must be someplace to run between the flames. Surely he'd found a way through to the other side... But Tracy was alone. How did she escape? The heat felt as if it would melt her even standing a few hundred yards away.

David had told her to run and get to safety, but safety was something she had felt only when she was at David's side. She couldn't run away and leave him behind. She bent over as racking coughs took control of her body.

Someone approached from behind. Tracy turned. Fearing it was Santino. Hoping it was David. But, no, it was a firefighter in full gear. He reached for Tracy, but she pulled away.

"David went that way. You have to save him."

The firefighter looked in the distance and shook his head, as if there was no hope of David surviving. He reached for Tracy again. She didn't want to go, but he tugged her with him, intent on getting her to safety.

"No!" Tracy yelled, reaching in the direction she'd seen David and Santino go.

But it was no use. The fireman carried her to safety.

At the Incident Command Center, Tracy stood in the parking lot, emergency vehicle lights blinking all around her. She tugged a blanket someone had thrown over her shoulders closer and stared at the fire blazing in the distance. It was consuming the side of the mountain and heading for the town, which could be yet another casualty of Santino's retaliation against Tracy.

The firefighters were creating a firebreak to save the town.

A backfire.

A fireman had saved her life, carried her to safety down a path she could never have found on her own to escape the flames. But David hadn't emerged, and she feared he'd perished in the flames trying to keep Santino away from her. And that was why she hadn't wanted to love. She couldn't stand to go through it all over again.

And yet here she was, reliving the nightmare.

How could Tracy live with this? Even if free will was to blame for Santino's actions, rather than God, how could she hold on to faith in a life where everything she loved was taken away from her?

Admittedly, she'd lost touch with God. Stopped praying as much as she should, when her reaction should have been the exact opposite. Seeing David's faith, and hearing the way he prayed, and his grandmother, too, had taught her that much. Reignited her own faith. But now it was faltering again.

She pulled the blanket around her tighter. When the smoke settled, literally, maybe things would look differently. And she knew in the end, God took bad things and turned them to good.

Tracy was still waiting to see good come of this.

That scripture from Isaiah 61 came to mind. Maybe because she'd recently seen it in a framed cross-stitch at Katy's house.

The Spirit of the Sovereign Lord is on me, because the Lord has anointed me to proclaim good news to the poor. He has sent me to bind up the brokenhearted, to proclaim freedom for the captives and release from darkness for the prisoners, to proclaim the year of the Lord's favor and the day of vengeance of our God, to comfort all who mourn, and provide for those who grieve in Zion—to bestow on them a crown of beauty instead of ashes, the oil of joy instead of mourning, and a garment of praise instead of a spirit of despair. They will be

*called oaks of righteousness, a planting of the Lord
for the display of his splendor.*

Tearing her gaze from the scene that had exploded and
expanded in front of her over the past couple of hours,
Tracy hung her head.

Beauty for ashes. That was what she needed. What they
all needed out of this.

*Lord, we definitely need the ruined cities—or in this
case, forest—repaired. We need those who have suffered
because of Santino to be comforted.*

When the gray of twilight tinted the skies in the wee
hours of an early Alaska morning, the flames still were
only partially contained. Tracy watched a figure emerge
from the smoke in the distance. She expected a fireman,
but the man wasn't wearing any gear. She feared Santino
had come for her.

But no. She knew that cadence. That set of his shoulders.

Her pulse ratcheted up and she dropped the blanket,
rushing forward. A man pulled her back— Adam, the
Warren brother who'd lost his business to fire just yester-
day and had arrived on the scene not long ago, along with
the other Warren siblings and Isaiah. Leah had stayed
behind with her new baby.

Right now she didn't want their interference. "But…
it's David."

"You know, I think you're right." Adam let her go.

Tracy hurried across the ground, closing the distance.
As she grew near, she saw David's stern features soften
into a smile when he saw her. Tracy jumped into his arms.
Covered in soot, he smelled of smoke and earth. He buried his face in her neck and shuddered.

She hadn't wanted to love again with good reason. But David's courage and bravery, his arms around her, brought her to her senses.

She *could* love again.

She *must* love again. Her heart would give her no other choice.

David finally released her, though she could have remained in his arms forever.

"I did it, Tracy. I saved the woman I love this time."

The look in his eyes, his words, made her heart flip-flop. "Love?"

"Yes, love."

Someone cleared a throat.

Tracy didn't want the interruption.

"Tracy. David." Chief Winters stood there, two US marshals next to him. "As soon as I learned where you were, and what had happened, we headed this way. Made it just in time, I see."

He introduced the marshals.

"Where's Jennifer…er…Marshal Hanes?" But Tracy feared she already knew.

"I was afraid we were too late," Chief Winters said. "I only just learned that Santino escaped tonight. Marshal Hanes was compromised, her family threatened, traumatized in such a way that she gave your location away. I'm sorry it took me so long to figure things out. But I had to know how you were discovered in Mountain Cove to begin with."

One of the marshals stepped forward. "I'm sorry, ma'am. But we'll handle things from here."

Reality forced its way into the moment. Tracy moved to step from David's arms. "I'm sorry, David. But you can't love me. I have to leave now. We talked about this.

It's the only way. I wish I had done this before I brought such havoc on everyone."

But David wouldn't let her go. "You don't have to go anywhere. Santino is dead."

Dizziness swept over her. She couldn't find words.

"How do you know?" Chief Winters asked.

"He tried to kill Tracy tonight, but I wouldn't let him. I chased him and we ended up nearly surrounded by a wall of fire. I escaped before it was too late." Weariness crept over his haggard features. "God help me, I tried to save him. Tried to pull him from the flames he'd stepped into. No matter what he'd done, I couldn't watch him die. But he…wouldn't let me help him. He thought he could save himself."

David hung his head. Tracy never wanted to see that look on his face again. He was a fireman and a hero. He never wanted to lose anyone—even someone who had committed heinous crimes. In the end, by fighting Santino, he'd saved Tracy.

Set her free.

"You saved me, David. You risked your life for me and saved me in the most important way."

"And I'd do it a hundred times over to keep you safe." David pressed his forehead against hers, oblivious to the US marshals and officials standing around them. "I only wish I hadn't avoided you for so long. I love you."

"I love you, too, David."

"Santino might be dead, Tracy," the marshal said, "but that doesn't negate efforts by his people. The door is still open for you to enter WITSEC, and I'm here to take you away to your new life."

How could she leave David? But then…how could she stay?

"Maybe a married name would help keep you under the radar," David said.

Tracy gasped.

"Will you marry me, Tracy?"

"Are you sure?" She wanted to make sure his proposal wasn't some sort of heroic act. "There's no need for you to go that far to save me."

He chuckled. "Then go that far to save me, Tracy, and marry me. I don't want to live without you."

"Yes. Oh, yes, David."

She had her beauty for ashes.

* * * * *

Dear Reader,

I hope you enjoyed reading *Backfire*. Tracy and David struggled with questions about why bad things happened in their lives, and I'm sure many of us struggle with those same questions. Sometimes we don't get the answers we want but I believe God is always there with us to answer our prayers and to turn things around, to trade beauty for ashes. I've seen Him do this in my own life too many times to count, so I can write this with confidence.

In writing Tracy's character, I kept questioning myself. Should I have her save herself? She seems too dependent on others and on the hero. Women don't need someone to save them anymore. I could have put a twist on the story. Have her save the hero instead.

The recent movie *Frozen* comes to mind. Disney has updated their damsel-in-distress stories, changing the princess in need of her prince to save her into a story in keeping with our modern thinking. I loved the movie, but to be honest, I see nothing wrong with a princess wanting her prince to save her. To rescue her. And when the princess is used to only depending on herself, sometimes the greatest act of bravery can be trusting someone else—letting yourself love someone else.

I find that very romantic, and in fact, the Bible as a whole is a romance story. Jesus even rides a white horse! He is our Prince come to save us. He laid down His life for us. So went my thinking in deciding to keep Tracy in need of help to keep the man from her traumatic past from killing her.

I love connecting with my readers. You can find ways to connect with me on my website. If you would like to get news about my upcoming titles, please sign up for my newsletter on my website: http://elizabethgoddard.com.

I pray God's many blessings on you!

Elizabeth Goddard

COMING NEXT MONTH FROM
Love Inspired® Suspense

Available July 7, 2015

DETECTING DANGER
Capitol K-9 Unit • by Valerie Hansen

The criminal Daniella Dunne once testified against is now free and setting off bombs around town. When Daniella's witness protection identity is compromised, she turns to capitol K-9 unit officer Isaac Black to prevent the explosive situation that's looming.

JOINT INVESTIGATION
Northern Border Patrol • by Terri Reed

A serial killer is on the loose, and Canadian Mountie Drew Kelley and FBI agent Sami Bennett reluctantly combine forces to bring the madman to justice. Chasing the killer across their nations' borders, Drew vows to protect his attractive partner at all costs.

EMERGENCY REUNION • by Sandra Orchard

After Sherri Steele is attacked in her ambulance, deputy Cole Donovan insists on safeguarding the stubborn paramedic. But when his brother becomes a suspect, he must choose between the love of his former crush or duty to his family.

HIGH-RISK HOMECOMING • by Alison Stone

When Ellie Winters discovers someone is running drugs through her new shop, FBI agent Johnny Rock is called in. Can the charming lawman from her past keep Ellie safe, or will her homecoming become short-lived?

HIDDEN IDENTITY • by Carol J. Post

Meagan Berry faked her death to escape an abusive relationship, but now the violent man has found her. Meagan must turn to handsome cop Hunter Kingston to keep her from an early grave.

HEADLINE: MURDER • by Maggie K. Black

Daniel Ash thought his days as a bodyguard were behind him, but he's thrown right back into the field when journalist Olivia Brant's investigative skills place her—and him—in a crime gang's sights.

LOOK FOR THESE AND OTHER LOVE INSPIRED BOOKS WHEREVER BOOKS ARE SOLD, INCLUDING MOST BOOKSTORES, SUPERMARKETS, DISCOUNT STORES AND DRUGSTORES.

LISCNM0615

REQUEST YOUR FREE BOOKS!

2 FREE RIVETING INSPIRATIONAL NOVELS PLUS 2 FREE MYSTERY GIFTS

Love Inspired®
SUSPENSE
RIVETING INSPIRATIONAL ROMANCE

YES! Please send me 2 FREE Love Inspired® Suspense novels and my 2 FREE mystery gifts (gifts are worth about $10). After receiving them, if I don't wish to receive any more books, I can return the shipping statement marked "cancel." If I don't cancel, I will receive 4 brand-new novels every month and be billed just $4.99 per book in the U.S. or $5.49 per book in Canada. That's a savings of at least 17% off the cover price. It's quite a bargain! Shipping and handling is just 50¢ per book in the U.S. and 75¢ per book in Canada.* I understand that accepting the 2 free books and gifts places me under no obligation to buy anything. I can always return a shipment and cancel at any time. Even if I never buy another book, the two free books and gifts are mine to keep forever.

123/323 IDN GH5Z

Name	(PLEASE PRINT)

Address	Apt. #

City	State/Prov.	Zip/Postal Code

Signature (if under 18, a parent or guardian must sign)

Mail to the **Reader Service:**
IN U.S.A.: P.O. Box 1867, Buffalo, NY 14240-1867
IN CANADA: P.O. Box 609, Fort Erie, Ontario L2A 5X3

**Are you a current subscriber to Love Inspired® Suspense books and want to receive the larger-print edition?
Call 1-800-873-8635 or visit www.ReaderService.com.**

* Terms and prices subject to change without notice. Prices do not include applicable taxes. Sales tax applicable in N.Y. Canadian residents will be charged applicable taxes. Offer not valid in Quebec. This offer is limited to one order per household. Not valid for current subscribers to Love Inspired Suspense books. All orders subject to credit approval. Credit or debit balances in a customer's account(s) may be offset by any other outstanding balance owed by or to the customer. Please allow 4 to 6 weeks for delivery. Offer available while quantities last.

Your Privacy—The Reader Service is committed to protecting your privacy. Our Privacy Policy is available online at www.ReaderService.com or upon request from the Reader Service.

We make a portion of our mailing list available to reputable third parties that offer products we believe may interest you. If you prefer that we not exchange your name with third parties, or if you wish to clarify or modify your communication preferences, please visit us at www.ReaderService.com/consumerchoice or write to us at Reader Service Preference Service, P.O. Box 9062, Buffalo, NY 14240-9062. Include your complete name and address.

"Capitol K-9 Unit Five, safety check at Washington Monument complete," Isaac Black radioed. "DC police are also on scene for crowd control."

"Copy," he heard echoed back into his earpiece. "Stand by."

Isaac turned his attention to Detective David Delvecchio of the DC Metro squad and smiled. "You look like something's bugging you. What's the matter?"

"I'm just not fond of congressmen who throw their weight around and cause unnecessary overtime." He eyed the news vans and cameramen surrounding Harland Jeffries. "If he wants to grandstand he should do it on his own turf."

"And preferably during office hours," Isaac added. He glanced down at Abby, his brown-and-white, bomb-detecting beagle. She had stretched out on the grassy verge skirting the Washington Monument, panting and cooling off after being excited doing her job. "At least one of us is happy to be working tonight."

"Yeah. I'm sure glad we have you and the rest of the K-9 team on call. My men didn't have time to do a proper sweep of this area. By the time we got the word about the congressman's impromptu press conference we only had an hour to deploy."

Isaac nodded. "Not to worry. If Abby says there's no bomb on the grounds, it's safe. You can trust her."

"I do," Delvecchio replied.

Curious tourists were gathering outside the police line, milling around and straining to get a peek at the action. Politicians and their aides in dark business suits stood out against the colorful garb of the bystanders like Secret Service agents would have at a three-ring circus performance.

Isaac was about to withdraw to his SUV and wait to be released when he noticed his dog stiffen and ease to her feet. Since he had not given the command, her actions drew his attention.

"Abby?" He crouched, following the beagle's line of sight. She was clearly focused on the small group nearest to the congressman. "What is it, girl?"

Instead of relaxing, the dog froze in place, her hackles bristling. Her nose quivered. Her tail was half-raised and still. If they had not just completed a search of the premises Isaac would think...

Isaac stood and grabbed the detective's sleeve. "Pull everybody back. Clear the area. Now!" Isaac's commanding tone left no doubt of his seriousness.

"Why? What do you see?"

"Nothing," Isaac said. "But Abby senses something's wrong, and that's good enough for me."

Don't miss
DETECTING DANGER by Valerie Hansen,
available July 2015 wherever
Love Inspired® Suspense books and ebooks are sold.

LISEXP0615